Velvet Whispers

Other Books By Joan Elizabeth Lloyd
Available From Carroll & Graf Publishers:

Black Satin

The Pleasure of JessicaLynn

Slow Dancing

The Love Flower

Velvet Whispers

by
Joan Elizabeth Lloyd

CARROLL & GRAF PUBLISHERS, INC.
NEW YORK

First Carroll & Graf edition 1999

Carroll & Graf Publishers, Inc.
19 West 21st Street
New York, NY 10010-6805

Library of Congress Cataloging-in-Publication Data is available.
ISBN: 0-7867-0640-6

Manufactured in the United States of America

Velvet Whispers

Chapter 1

"Hi, Sugar." Liza's voice was soft and husky, not its usual speaking tone. "How's my man tonight?" She had also added just a hint of a southern accent, which softened and lengthened each word.

"I'm just great now that I can hear your voice, Liza."

Liza shifted the phone to her other shoulder and settled back into her overstuffed lounge chair in the small room that was her private space. "I'm so thrilled that you called."

"You knew I would. It's Tuesday, you know."

"I do know, but sometimes you are really naughty and disappoint me." She had already double-checked to be sure that the door was closed and locked and now she reached up and turned off the light. The room was now lit only by mid-evening moonlight shining through the window. She could close the blinds, but Liza liked the softening effect the moonlight had on her psyche. "I just hate it when you're naughty."

"I like being naughty with you, Liza," the man purred.

"Mmm," she purred back. "Maybe we should be naughty together. What should we do?"

After a slight pause, he said, "Let's take a walk in the woods."

"Good idea." Liza created her picture of him, walking beside her between tall trees, the air filled with the smell of pine. He was tall, with broad shoulders, long fingers, a broad chest, and narrow hips. Mentally she created his face, all planes and angles, with a firm jaw and soft lips. His eyes were deep blue with raven lashes that matched the long wavy black hair he wore gathered at the nape of his neck with a leather thong. "Yes, let's," she said. "Will you hold my hand?"

"Oh yes," the man said, his voice soft yet clear despite the miles between them.

"It's so cool here in the shade of the trees, but your hand is warm, and I can feel the heat travel up my arm warming all of me. Are you warm too?" She felt in the near darkness for the glass of wine she had placed on the table beside her chair and took a silent sip. As she always did, she felt a delicious tingle all over.

"You know I am," he said.

"It's so quiet here," she continued. She lifted her long hair from the back of her neck and draped it over the back of the chair. "Our footsteps are almost completely silent on the deep carpet of pine needles. I can hear a bird far away, its song faint and almost melancholy. The sky is so blue that it almost hurts my eyes. The breeze is cool, but the pockets of bright sun are warm and each time we walk from shadow to brightness, I turn my face up to the heat and feel it through my body."

"What are you wearing? Tell me how you look."

She already knew his preferences. "Well, you know that you're tall enough to tower over me. I like having to look up to see your handsome face. I'm wearing my hair in a single braid down my back, and there's only a slender black ribbon at the bottom holding it together. It will be easy to remove."

"And the rest of you?"

Liza could hear his breathing, now a bit heavy. "I'm wearing a peasant blouse of soft white cotton. It's been washed so many times that the fabric is almost transparent. And I have on that full, dark green skirt that I know you like so much and soft leather sandals. I'm afraid that I had so little time to dress this morning that I didn't put on anything underneath my clothes. It's a bit embarrassing."

"Oh, baby," the man said, "you know me too well."

"I'm afraid that from your height, you can see right down the front of my blouse. I can't help it if the cool wind makes my nipples hard. I hope you won't look."

There was a soft chuckle. "Of course I won't look," he said.

In her chair, Liza unbuttoned her blouse and slid her palm over her satin-covered breasts. In the dark she almost became the girl in the woods. "I'm so glad I can trust you that way. Let's walk for a ways. I know there's a small stream just over that little hill. If we're feeling brave, we can wade through the cold water to the big flat rock in the middle. It will be a nice place for us to sit and talk." She was silent for a moment, then continued. "Do you like it here? Of course you do. I knew you'd like this place. The sun is shining through the branches of the huge trees that line the stream and, as the wind blows softly, the sunlight sparkles on the smoothly flowing water. Shall we cross to that rock?"

"Oh yes. We really should."

"Good. But you wouldn't want to ruin your beautiful leather boots, would you? Sit down here on the bank and take them off. Shall I help you? Of course I should. I'll just unlace them. You know it's hard for me to keep my hands off your muscular thighs, but I'm a bit embarrassed and I really shouldn't touch you."

"It's all right. You can touch me." His voice was hoarse with excitement.

"Are you sure?"

His "Yes" was no more than a long-drawn-out sigh.

"Oh, your legs are so hard and tight and sexy," she said. "I love to slide just the tips of my fingers over your knees and then up your beautiful thighs. I want to touch that large bulge at the front of your pants, but I don't dare, so I'll stop my hands and just pull off your boots. Why don't you take your shirt off, too, so you can enjoy the warm sunshine?"

"Will you take your blouse off too?"

"Sugar, I knew you were a naughty boy." She paused. "You are so beautiful without your shirt. Your chest is hairless and so smooth. Your abdomen is rippled with muscles so hard, I just love to touch it." She laughed. "No, I shouldn't do that. Instead, I'm going to kick off my sandals and run through the water to the big flat rock out in the middle of the stream. Can you see it?"

"Yes."

"Ooh, it's hard to climb out of the water onto this rock. The stones in the stream are mossy and quite slippery. Okay, I've got a hold now. Good. I can sit on top. Mmm. The rock is almost hot from the sun. I've left wet footprints on the stone. Are you coming? I can see you standing there on the stream bank, so handsome and sexy. I'll pull my blouse off over my head if you want so you can see my large breasts. I'll just put it over here. Do you like the way I look?"

"Yes. I'm going to wade to your rock."

"I'm going to remove the ribbon from my hair. I run my fingers through it and pull my brown curls over my chest, but they don't quite keep my nipples from poking through.

They're so hard and tight. I guess it's from thinking about you and your gorgeous body." She sighed deeply. "I'm going to lie down on the warm stone. Oh yes. I can feel the heat against the bare skin of my back. Do you need any help climbing onto the rock?"

"Not at all. I like being here with you."

"It's good to have you here beside me now." She paused. "Oh, look. You've gotten the bottoms of your pants legs wet. Why don't you take your pants off and lay them out on the rock so they can dry? Come on, take them off. No one can see." She paused for a heartbeat. "There. Isn't that better? Oh, my," she said. "You're not wearing anything under those pants, you naughty boy. Lie down on your back and let the rock warm your tight buttocks. Shall I warm you too?"

"Mmm," his voice purred.

"Maybe I'll just cuddle against you with my breasts pressed against your chest. Can you feel my hard nipples against your smooth skin? The contrast between the cool breeze and the warm sun is so exciting. And we're here in the open. If any people come by, they'll know what we're doing. Do we care?"

"Of course not. We just care about each other."

"That's so wonderful. I love the feel of you. May I kiss you?"

"Oh yes."

"Your mouth is so soft, yet strong. Part your lips so I can taste you. You taste so good." She waited just a moment. "You don't know what I'm doing. I've got my fingers in the cold water and now I'm going to drip icy water on your swollen shaft. Oooh, that's cold. Shall I warm it with my mouth?"

"Oh, God."

"Your cock is so hard it's standing straight up, urging me to take it between my lips. When I open my mouth wide, I can barely take all of you. I'm doing my best to surround your cock with my hot, wet mouth and I can suck most of you inside. You taste so good. I pull you deep into my mouth, then draw back, over and over until that cock is so hard it's almost painful. Now I'm sitting up, watching you stare at my body. I know how much you want me. You want to grab me, but I know you won't. You're so patient and you let me set the pace."

"But I'm so hungry."

"I know and I'll bet that the cool air on your wet cock feels *sooo* sexy. Would you like to suck my nipples?" Liza sighed and pulled her bra cups down and pinched her own erect nipples. The picture in her head was making her really hot.

"I love sucking you," he said.

"Yes. Suck me. I'm going to climb over you so my big breasts hang over your mouth. Don't raise your head. Let me do it. I slowly lower my breast until the nipple brushes your lips. Now open your mouth. Yes, like that." She pinched again and felt the shards of pleasure rocket through her. "I love it when you suck me, but that's not enough for me now. I need you inside me. Your large cock will fill me so completely. I'm going to move lower and touch your rigid staff with my wet pussy. Then I'll spread my skirt so that it covers us both. No one can see the secrets we hide beneath the dark green cotton. I've got the tip of you against my wetness. Do you want to be inside?"

"Oh, God. Oh, God."

"Not too fast. I like it really slow. Millimeter by millimeter I lower myself onto you. My body's so hot and wet. Do you want to thrust into me? I know you do, but be patient. Let me go *sooo* slowly until you fill me completely. Yes, like that," she purred. Without changing her voice pattern, she unzipped her jeans and wiggled them down over her hips. Then she inserted her fingers between her thighs and rubbed

her bottom against the soft leather of the chair. "Like that."
She found her clit and rubbed. "Just like that. If we keep
doing that, I'm going to come. Are you?"

"Yes," he said, his breathing now rapid and raspy.

"I'm raising up on my knees and then dropping suddenly onto your stiff cock. Over and over I raise and lower."
She rubbed. "Just a few more times. Do it for me. Drive that
big cock of yours into my hungry body." With the help of
her experienced fingers, Liza came.

"Yes," the man said. "Just another moment." He paused,
then groaned. "Yes," he whispered.

Liza panted, the telephone lying against her shoulder.
"That was wonderful, as always, sugar."

"Yes, it was. Maybe I can call you again next Tuesday."

"I'll look forward to hearing from you."

A hundred miles away, the man hung up the phone then
took a tissue and wiped the semen from his liver-spotted
hand and his now-flaccid cock. As he stretched back on
his bed he thought about his wife of forty-three years, now
gone for more than two. *I used to be like that man in
Liza's story,* he thought, *and Myra was like the woman, so
hot and receptive. Oh, baby, I miss you so much,* he
thought, *but Liza fills some of the emptiness and I know
you wouldn't mind.*

Bless Liza.

Bless Velvet Whispers.

⌒

Alice Waterman rubbed the back of her neck, trying to
loosen what had become a semipermanent kink. Had it
always been there? she wondered. No, she suspected, only
for the past few months, since her mother had taken ill. She
glanced up and peered through the square opening above

her desk as the office's outer door opened and closed. A man of about fifty crossed the waiting room and casually leaned on the sill of Alice's window. "Good morning, Mr. McGillis," Alice said, making sure both her voice and her face were cheerful. Dental patients were always a bit tense and she knew that her cheery attitude tended to relax them just a bit.

"Good morning, Alice. How are you this morning?"

"I'm fine. How about you?"

"I'm okay."

"How's your son? Did you hear about medical school?"

Mr. McGillis's face lit up. "It's so nice of you to remember. Yes, we're very excited. He was accepted to Johns Hopkins, of all places. We're going to miss him terribly, but it's his first choice and he's thrilled. We never expected him to get in, even with his terrific grades."

Alice made it a point to remember details about the patients' lives, further putting them at ease. "That's great news. Congratulate him for all of us." She winked. "And be sure he comes in for his checkup before he leaves."

"I will."

"Dr. Tannenbaum will be with you in just a moment. He's just finishing up with his previous patient." The woman whose painful molar was being filled had been almost fifteen minutes late and now Dr. Tannenbaum would be a bit behind all morning.

"No problem," Mr. McGillis said. "I'll wait as long as necessary. Years even."

Alice chuckled. "I'm sure it won't be that long." She flipped the switch that would turn on the doctor's "The Next Patient Is Waiting" light in the rear operatory. As she watched, Mr. McGillis took a well-thumbed magazine from the rack and settled into a soft upholstered chair. As Alice returned to her computer, her best friend, Betsy, one of Dr. Tannenbaum's dental assistants, settled into a chair beside her. "He's almost done." Betsy shook her head slowly. "That woman's going to be the death of me," she said, sotto voce referring to Mrs. Sutter, the woman with the painful molar. "First she's late and then she's irritated that we won't sit and chat. 'Let me tell you about my granddaughter,' she says. 'She's just started walking. . . .' Then she drags out about fifty pictures." When Alice failed to react, Betsy said, "Earth to Alice. Where are you?"

Alice refocused her deep brown eyes. "Sorry. I guess I'm really preoccupied this morning."

"I gathered that when you almost charged Mr. Cardova for a root canal when all he had was a cleaning. You never do that. Anything I can help you with?"

Alice and Betsy had been friends off and on since high school. Seated alphabetically, Alice Waterman and Betsy York had been relegated to the far back of the room, free to whisper and giggle, mostly about boys and the constant bulge beneath their social studies teacher Mr. Hollingsworth's trousers. "I'm afraid not," Alice said softly. Then she sighed, knowing that Betsy really cared. "It looks like my sister and I are going to have to put Mom in a nursing home." Alice's sister, Susan, was six years older, married with a teenaged daughter. Although their mother's illness had brought them a bit closer, she and her sister had little in common.

Betsy reached out and took Alice's small hand in her large one. "Oh, hon, I'm so sorry. Your mom's really that bad?"

"She keeps having more small strokes and she's really out of it. Sue called me last night and said that the doctor's recommending twenty-four-hour care. Sue can be home with her for a few days and she's got a friend who can baby-sit for a few weeks. We can pay her about twenty-five dollars a day and she'll be happy to earn it. But she can only do it until the first of May when she moves, so in about six weeks, we'll have no choice but to find a nursing home for Mom."

Alice thought about her mother, always a robust woman until four months earlier when she had her first "episode" as the doctor put it. She had collapsed in the kitchen of her New York City apartment. Sue, Alice's sister, had phoned and gotten no answer so, after several hours, Sue had called the police. Their "check on the welfare" visit had ultimately resulted in the superintendent opening the apartment door and the ambulance screaming Mrs. Waterman away.

After three more mini strokes the woman who had raised and cared for her two daughters was now in need of permanent care herself. Alice had visited her at her sister's house in Queens just last weekend, making the long drive south to spend time with the woman who was now only a shadow of the person she used to be. As Alice had walked into her niece's bedroom, now taken over by the seriously ill older woman, her mother had smiled just a bit and her eyes had softened. Alice had sat, holding her hand and talking to her for more than an hour, until her mother fell asleep.

Betsy's indigo eyes expressed her deep concern more than any words could. "Do you have a place in mind? I hear the Rutlandt Nursing Home down-county is really pretty good."

"We've been asking around since Mom's first stroke and Sue and I would love to have her there. It's halfway between us and would be so convenient for visiting. It's supposed to be first-rate, but it costs the earth." She sighed. She'd been over it and over it and there was just no way. "We'll just have to find something more within our price range. We're going out to look again this weekend." She pictured her mother sharing a gray-painted room with some other incapacitated woman, being patted on the head, fed and cleaned, but otherwise ignored. *No,* she thought, *I can't dwell on that.* Alice grinned ruefully. "I could always win the lottery."

Rutlandt had bright colors on the walls and nurses who cared, really cared. When she and Sue had visited, an elderly man was being wheeled to a waiting ambulance on a stretcher. One nurse kissed him good-bye. Kissed him like she cared. If they could only swing it. With a child of their own, Sue and her husband were only going to be able to add a small amount to her mother's Social Security and her late-father's pension and insurance payments. Alice could manage only a few dollars as well and neither family had any savings to speak of. With just a hundred dollars a week more, they could manage it. Sure, she thought. A hundred extra dollars a week. It might as well be a million.

"You don't ever play the lottery," Betsy said.

Alice returned to her friend. "Yeah. Makes it harder, doesn't it."

Despite Alice's sad news, Betsy grinned. "You never lose your sense of humor, do you?"

"I try to keep it light, but this really has me down." Alice glanced up and assured herself that Mr. McGillis was still reading his magazine. Then she combed her stubby fingers through deep-brown hair that she wore cut short so she needed to do nothing after her morning shower but rub it dry with a towel. The extra fifteen pounds she carried was evenly distributed over her five-foot-three-inch frame and, although she wore a size sixteen, her uniform, a loose, brightly patterned scrub top and white pants, covered most of the extra weight. "So many of those places are so awful; ugly places where people go who are already dead but their bodies haven't gotten the final message yet. It's just so depressing." She tapped her forehead. "Although she can't speak, Mom's brain's still alive and I hate to see her relegated to nothingness."

A "Green" light lit on the panel on the wall, indicating that Betsy could bring Mr. McGillis back into the operatory. "You know," Betsy said rising, "I might have a solution to your problem. Can you stop by my house right after work? It's time I filled you in on a little secret."

Alice had little time to wonder what Betsy was talking about, as Mrs. Sutter bustled out of the back room. "Wait till you see. I've got new pictures of Christine."

"That's wonderful, Mrs. Sutter. I can't wait to see them."

At five-fifteen, Dr. Tannenbaum closed his office and Alice and Betsy walked down the staircase and across the parking lot. "Don't forget," Betsy said, "you're going to stop by at the house."

"Okay," Alice said, rubbing the back of her neck. "I'll see you there." She climbed behind the wheel of her seven-year-old Toyota and started the engine. It was late March and the willow trees in Putnam County, New York, had just started to get that wonderful green glow that signaled the beginning of spring. It had been a particularly cold winter, and the season had yet to loosen its hold. The forsythia were still trying to bloom with just a few errant blossoms coloring the slender, leafless branches. Two-sythia her mother used to call them. Alice sighed and tried not to think about the older woman.

The weather forecaster on Channel 2 had said that the weekend should bring a dramatic rise in temperature. As she shifted into drive, Alice wondered whether she could drive down to Sue's and take her mother out, if only in a wheelchair. But where would they get one? Could they afford one? They must cost a fortune. Maybe through Medicare or maybe they could rent one.

"Stop it," Alice said out loud. "You're making yourself crazy." She turned up the volume on the radio and sang along with the Five Satins. "Show dote 'n showbee-doe. Show dote 'n showbee-doe. In the still . . ." By the time she pulled into Betsy's driveway behind her friend's new Buick, her spirits had lightened considerably.

The two women got out of their cars and walked up the well-tended front walk. "I can't wait for the azaleas," Betsy said. "It's like everything's holding its breath waiting for the temperature to go up."

"I know. The weatherman says this weekend."

"God, it's a hell-of-about time." She opened the front door and yelled, "I'm home."

Shouts of "Hi, Mom" were followed by three pair of feet pounding down the stairs. "Mom, Justin says that Mr. Marks is going to let him play third base this year. That's mine. Mr. Marks promised last spring he'd let me play third."

"Mom," another voice yelled, "can I go to the mall tonight? Everyone's going to be there."

"Mom," a third boy called, "can you quiz me on my spelling words?"

"Hold it!" Betsy yelled. "Alice and I need fifteen minutes of peace and quiet, then all things will work out."

"Oh, hi Alice," Betsy's three look-alike boys said almost in unison.

"Hi, guys. If you all need an extra chauffeur later, I can help."

"Thanks, Alice," Josh, Betsy's twelve-year-old, said.

"Okay, guys," Betsy said in her best motherly voice. "Is there anything that can't wait fifteen minutes? If not, shoo." She made pushing motions toward the staircase.

After several long-suffering sighs and a small amount of grumbling, the three boys disappeared back upstairs. "Now," Betsy said, making her way into the kitchen, "how about a soda?"

"Love it. I'm really dry." Alice dropped into a kitchen chair. "I've only been here five minutes and already your boys have me exhausted. How do you do it?"

"I haven't got a clue. They say that if a cowboy starts lifting a calf at birth and picks him up each day, eventually he'll be able to lift an entire cow. I think I'm lifting a cow now—or maybe three."

Betsy put two glasses of Diet Coke on the table and settled into the chair opposite Alice. "Now, let me tell you something about me you don't know. I hope you're not going to be mad that I've been keeping secrets but at first it didn't seem that important. Then it got bigger and I didn't know how to tell you."

"You don't have to tell me anything you don't want to, you know," Alice said. "But I must admit that you've got me curious. Do you rob banks in your spare time? Do you rent the boys out for white slavery?"

The corners of Betsy's mouth tried to curve upward, but didn't quite make it. She started to speak, then turned it into a deep sigh.

Alice reached over and took her friend's hand. "Hey. Whatever it is, it's not tragic. It will work out. Really."

Betsy clasped Alice's hand. "It's not like that at all. It's wonderful, the most fun I've ever had, but it's weird. I'm just not sure how you'll take it."

Alice took a swallow of her soda. "I'm really intrigued. Why don't you just spit it out?"

"I have another job one evening a week."

"Really, I never knew." Seeing Betsy's face, she knew there was more. "And . . ."

"I do phone sex."

"What?"

"I do phone sex. My name's Liza, or whatever the customer wants it to be, and I talk to them. You know, hot, erotic stuff."

"You're joking. What do you really do?"

Betsy withdrew her hand and sipped her Coke. "That's what I really do. I work one night a week for three hours and I average between two hundred and two hundred and fifty dollars."

"You're serious." Alice's mind was boggled. Betsy had always seemed so straight. So white-picket-fence. Three handsome boys and a great-looking husband. "What does Larry think about this? Does he know?"

"Of course he knows. Every Tuesday evening I disappear into the den, stretch out in the lounge chair, and take my calls. It works out well because the office is closed on Wednesdays, so if I run late, I can catch a nap the next day while the boys are at school."

"I have only a million questions. Do the boys know?"

"No. Of course not. They know I'm in phone sales, and that's enough. They know that on Tuesday evenings I work in the den and I'm not to be disturbed."

"How long have you been doing this? How did you start? How does it work? Do you have regular customers?" Alice leaned forward. "I mean, it just doesn't seem like you. I mean, phone sex. Shit. I'm babbling."

Betsy smiled softly. "How about this? Larry won't be home until late tonight. If you've got no plans for dinner, let's take the boys out for pizza at the mall and we can talk then. It will also give you some time to digest what I just told you. We can then send Phillip and Bran to the arcade for a while and Josh can spend time with his friends. While they're gone, I'll answer any questions you've got. Yes?"

"Sure." Alice shook her head as if trying to get puzzle pieces to fit. They wouldn't. Not a chance.

Ten minutes later, the five of them stood in Betsy's driveway. "Alice," Brandon, Betsy's nine-year-old said, "can I ride with you? You could test me on my spelling. And I've got to be able to use the words in sentences. You could come up with a story."

Alice had always believed that learning could be fun and she had developed a game with the boys. They would give her a group of words and she would come up with a story that used them all. They would hand the tale off, one to the other, each adding a paragraph wilder than the previous to try to stump the next storyteller.

"Sure, if that's okay with everyone else."

"I love your stories," Josh said. "Can I come too?"

"That sounds great," Betsy said. "Phillip, you can ride with me and we'll talk about third base."

Chapter 2

When they reached the mall, the two women parked next to each other and the boys piled out. "That was a great one, Alice," Josh said. "Phillip, you should have heard the story we did." He insinuated himself between his brother and his mother. "It was fantastic, Mom, with monsters and people on another planet." With Phillip in the lead, the three boys ran ahead toward Festival of Italy.

"Thanks for taking Josh and Bran. It gave me a chance to have a heart-to-heart with Phillip about the Little League team."

"You're welcome. I really enjoy your kids, and the stories we get into tax my creativity sometimes. Bran had the word *gravity* on his vocabulary list so we got into life on Mars. Each time one of the boys took a turn, the story got more fantastic."

"It's that imagination of yours that intrigues me." They walked through the mall entrance. "We'll talk about it later."

They sat down at a large table in the pizza parlor and, after considerable argument, agreed on a small pie with pepperoni and a small with half mushrooms, half extra cheese. "Don't let them get any mushrooms on my side," Brandon said. "Yuck."

"There will be none of that," Betsy said.

"Can we continue the story, Alice?" Brandon asked. "Maybe Josh can have a turn."

"Not me," Josh said, eyeing a table filled with other kids about his age. "Storytelling's too babyish for me."

"But, Josh," Bran said.

"It's all right, Bran," Alice said. "I understand completely. He doesn't have to join in unless he wants to. We can do a great story without him. Maybe we'll even let your mother take a turn."

"I'm getting to be a pretty good storyteller and Phil's terrific," Betsy said, rubbing Phil's hair. "Fill the kid and me in."

For the next half an hour the group tossed the tale back and forth, taxing their collective imaginations. After wolfing down three slices, Josh had moved to the table with his friends, but the other four were more than able to complete the fantastic story.

"So finally Morg got the ray gun and blasted everyone," Phil said. "Then he climbed back into his spaceship and headed for Earth."

"The end," Alice said.

"No," Bran whined, "don't make it end."

Betsy reached into her wallet and handed each boy a five-dollar bill. "How about you two go over to the arcade while Alice and I visit? We'll meet you at the main entrance in . . ."

"An hour?" the two boys chorused.

"Let's make it half an hour. In the meantime in case you need us, Alice and I will be sitting on the benches right outside the arcade. I want you two to stay together. If I see either of you alone, that will be the end."

"Make it forty-five minutes," Phillip said.

"Okay. Forty-five minutes it is." The two boys dashed off and Betsy walked over to Josh, bent down, and whispered in his ear. Then she stood, raised an eyebrow and her son nodded.

"Okay," Betsy said as she rejoined her friend. "We're clear until seven-thirty. How about we get cappuccinos and sit and talk?"

Hot, frothy coffee in hand, the two women found an unoccupied bench near the arcade and made themselves comfortable. "You've been mysterious long enough," Alice said, sipping her hot coffee. "Tell me everything."

"Do you remember when I was so depressed a few years after Brandon was born? I felt lousy about myself. I couldn't work with three boys and I felt like a slug."

"Yeah. That was a really bad time for you but you pulled yourself out of it, as I remember."

"I started working with Velvet."

"Velvet?"

"Velvet Polaski. Velvet Whispers. That's the agency through which I get the customers." Betsy hesitated. "This is really awkward. It's tough to tell your best friend that you've had a secret for six years. I'm not sure I know how you'll react to this whole thing even now."

Alice stared at her friend, wondering how you could be best friends with someone for almost fifteen years and not know something that seemed so important. Velvet Whispers. "Hey, I love you," Alice said. "You're my oldest and dearest friend. There's nothing you could tell me that would change that."

"I hope so. It all goes back to the night Brandon was born. I went into labor at about midnight but I didn't call you until the next morning. You had had the flu and were still a bit rocky, and maybe contagious. Remember? And of course Larry had to stay home with the two older boys."

"I do remember and I still feel guilty about it all. I should have baby-sat so that Larry could have been with you."

"Actually it was a blessing in disguise. I didn't mind being at the hospital by myself. After all, Brandon was my third and I hadn't had bad labors with the other two. I had a book so, for a while, between contractions, I read and watched the clock. At about 2:00 A.M., another woman came in and they put us together in one labor room, I guess to keep each other company. I think the labor-and-delivery area was really crowded and all the birthing suites were full. Nurses kept running in, checking on us and dashing out again."

Betsy sipped her coffee, then continued. "Anyway. This woman and I got to talking as we tried not to concentrate on the pains. What else was there to do, after all? Her name was Victoria, but everyone called her Velvet. The baby was her first and she was very nervous. Her husband was away on a business trip and, with no real family, I became the calm expert, the voice of reason. I helped her along, sort of told her what to expect. We got quite chummy, quite quickly. Between pains, there was a strange sense of intimacy. We talked about our husbands, my kids, like that."

Betsy's mind drifted back to parts of that strange conversation.

"Do you work?" Velvet had asked.

"With a two-and-a-half-year-old and a sixteen-month-old, I sure do."

"Sorry," Velvet said. "Dumb question."

"Actually, I did work before the boys were born. I'm a dental assistant." Betsy sighed. "I guess I miss it. When your world is populated by gremlins two feet tall who speak only single words, it gets a bit boring."

"I'll bet. I'm going to keep my job after the baby. I just can't give it up."

"What do you do?" Betsy asked.

"I'm in phone sales."

"What do you sell?"

Just then a contraction interrupted Velvet's conversation. When the pain subsided, she said, "I sell sex."

Betsy sat bolt upright. "Come again?"

"I have a phone-sex business. Men call and I talk to them. I'm really busy and I make quite a good living."

"You're kidding." Betsy looked at her new friend, and saw that Velvet was totally serious. "Okay. You're not kidding."

"No. I'm not. It started as a joke several years ago with some buddies of my husband's. They wanted to play a prank on one of their friends so they set me up to talk dirty to him. They thought it would be a lark, but, as they listened in, they realized that I was very good at it. Actually, I felt bad about it, playing such a joke, but he was a great guy and let me off the hook."

The two women stopped talking as Velvet had another contraction, making conversation impossible. When things calmed, Velvet continued, "I was so good at it that, secretly, one of Bob's friends kept calling, asking me to talk dirty to him. I did, and he paid me."

"He actually paid you?"

"Fifty bucks for half an hour. He said that's what he paid for other phone-sex lines and that I deserved every penny of it. He told someone, and they told others. Now I have men calling every night and I make a nice living. It's too bad I'll have to cut back now, with the baby and all."

Betsy turned to Alice. "So Velvet and I had our babies and crossed paths a few times that first year at the pediatrician's office. She loved motherhood and our babies both thrived. It was a couple of years later, when I was so depressed, that I ran into her again at the pediatrician's office." Betsy sipped her cappuccino. "We got to talking. Dr. Brewster was running late, as usual, so we had almost an hour to visit. It was quite a while before I asked her about the business."

When Betsy drifted off, Alice prodded. "And?"

"Business was booming and Velvet had hired another woman to answer calls but she was still having to turn away customers. When she heard that I was so down, she suggested that I give her business a try. I was horrified, of course, but, well, as time passed, the idea began to appeal to me somehow. I discussed it with Larry and he was all for it. Things between us have always been great and he thought I'd be good at talking dirty to men. He was also glad that I seemed to be perking up. A phone-based job wouldn't entail having to travel to work and he promised to take care of the kids one evening a week. Both the money and something to do were welcome."

People walked past their bench, but the two women were oblivious. "How did this Velvet know you'd be good at phone sex? Wasn't she taking a risk?"

"Actually she had a friend call me and be my first customer just to be sure, but after so many years on the phone, she's a pretty good judge of character."

"I couldn't have done it," Alice said, putting her coffee on the bench beside her.

"Needless to say, I was terrified, but after a few moments I guess I just got into it."

"Tell me about it," Alice urged.

"His name was Austin. Velvet had given me some reading to do, some ideas for how to talk to men. She'd also let me listen to her end of a few conversations. That made me feel better but I quickly learned that every call and every client is different."

"So Austin called you. Weren't you scared with him having your phone number?"

"She had given me his number and I called him at a pre-arranged time. Velvet pays me and covers my phone bill too."

"What about the real customers?"

"They call and give credit-card information to a router, who finds out what the client wants, then relays the call. Velvet doesn't take many calls anymore so she usually does that herself. Sometimes, if she's busy, one of us goes to her place and does it."

"One of us?"

"There are almost a dozen women working for her now. She pays us fifty dollars an hour for routing, and on the phone we get half of whatever Velvet charges."

"Wow, I never imagined."

"Neither did I that first time."

"Do you remember that first call?"

At that moment, Phillip dashed out of the arcade. "Mom, Bran's hogging the Duel of Death. It's my turn."

"You know the rules," Betsy said. "If you can't work out your problems, we're out of here."

"But Mom . . ."

Betsy raised an eyebrow and Phillip slunk back into the arcade. The two women clearly heard him yell, "Bran, Mom says . . ."

Chuckling, the two women returned to their conversation. "That first call," Betsy said. "How could I ever forget? I had told Larry all about it and he was incredulous, but willing to go along, especially since I was going to get paid. He said he'd put the boys to bed, then watch a ball game in the living room and that I should come down when I was done. I was supposed to call the guy at about eight so I locked myself in the bedroom at about seven-thirty and shook for half an hour."

Betsy sat in her small bedroom, alternately exhilarated and terrified. *What's the worst that can happen?* she asked herself. *So I make an idiot of myself. So I'm so tongue-tied that I can't speak at all. So what?* At exactly eight, she looked down at the small sheet of paper on which Velvet had written the number and reread it, although she had already memorized it. Velvet had said that she might want to extend the call as long as possible since she was being paid by the hour, but Betsy had rejected that idea. The call would last as long as it lasted and she'd make what she made. She wouldn't con anyone. When she had apologized to Velvet, the woman had laughed. That was her theory too.

Hands trembling, Betsy picked up the phone and dialed. "Hello?"

Betsy had a naturally soft, slightly husky voice and Velvet had told her that she needn't change anything. "Hello. I'm glad I could call you tonight." She tried to sit on the edge of the bed, but found that she needed to pace while she talked.

"I'm glad you could too," he said. "My name's Austin. What's yours?"

"What would you like my name to be?" So far, so good. She was following the pattern she had set up for herself. The standard, as Velvet had told her, was to let the man lead the way as much as possible.

"I don't know. How about Mona?"

"Okay. Mona it is. What are you wearing, Austin?"

"Just jeans and a polo shirt."

"What color shirt? I want to be able to picture you."

"It's yellow."

"Is it tight, so I can see your chest and arms as the shirt hugs you?"

"Yes," he said with a sigh. "What are you wearing?"

Betsy was actually wearing a comfortable sweat suit, but she answered, "I'm wearing a tank top that's slightly too small for me, and a pair of shorts."

"Are you wearing underwear?"

"Oh yes, but we can take them off together." Betsy listened carefully to the sound of Austin's breathing as Velvet had suggested, to gauge how excited he was. So far, he was pretty calm. She settled on the edge of the bed.

"Do you have shoes on?" he asked.

Betsy toed at her sneakers. "I do, but I can kick them off so my bare toes can wiggle. Would you like me to do that?"

"Oh yes," Austin said. "I want to hear you kick them off."

Betsy used the toe of one foot to ease her sneaker off her heel then bent over and held the phone near the floor as she pushed it off and it dropped on the rug. "I'm afraid you didn't hear much," she said, "since there's a nice thick rug. Let me kick off the other one." Again she moved the phone so Austin could hear the thud. "Now I can wiggle my bare toes in the carpet. It's so soft." Betsy could hear Austin's sigh. Although Velvet hadn't told her so, Austin might like feet, she thought, filing the knowledge away. She'd done a lot of reading, hoping that nothing could surprise her.

"I like that. I'm going to kick my shoes off too. Hear that?" She heard the slap of shoe sole on hard floor.

"It sounds like you don't have a carpet there," she said. "That's too bad. If you did you could walk barefoot on the soft rug as we talk."

"I wish I could do that too."

"Here's an idea. Why don't you get a thick towel from the bathroom and spread it on the cold floor? Then we can both walk around as we talk."

Betsy could hear Austin's excitement. "What a great idea. Hold on." The line went silent. Betsy took a deep breath. So far, so good.

"He actually got a towel?" Alice asked. "How did you think to do that?"

"I haven't a clue. It just came to me. Most of my calls now are spontaneous. I have no idea from one moment to the next what direction they will take."

"I'm still flabbergasted."

"You know, me too. I still can't believe I do this, but it's so much fun now."

"Back then it must have been really scary."

"Believe me, it was."

Austin returned to the phone. "I'm back, and I have a towel on the floor. I can curl my toes, and it's so soft."

"Good. Let's walk as we talk." Betsy was momentarily tongue-tied and the silence started to drag. *What can I say now?* she screamed at herself. *I have to get to sexy stuff.* "You know," she said inspired, "it's really hot in my room here."

"It is?"

"Yes. I'd like to take my sweater off."

"You mean your tank top."

"Right." Dumb. Dumb. She took the piece of paper with the phone number on it and wrote *tank top and shorts. Barefoot.* "It's a knit top and it's red. Bright red. I love red. Do you? Can you picture my bright red tank top?"

"Yes, Mona, I can," he said, "but take it off. Tell me about your bra."

Betsy jotted the word *Mona* on her pad. It wouldn't do for her to forget the name Austin had given her. "Well," she said, trying to sound as if she was removing her clothing, "it's red too. And it's lace, with thin straps."

"Are your breasts big?"

She remembered that Velvet had suggested that she always have large breasts. "Do you like big breasts?"

"Yes. I love tits that fill my hands."

"How would you like them to look?"

"Oh, they'd be white, with big, really dark nipples, and the nipples would be sticking out."

"How strange?" Betsy said. "You've just described me really well. I have a bit of a tan, but my tits are really white.

I never sunbathe topless since someone might see my boobs." *Yes,* she thought, *use those hot words.*

"Can I see them?" There was a long pause. "Please."

"I guess. Let me unhook my bra. I'm cradling the phone against my ear now so I can reach around and get at the hooks."

"It doesn't hook at the front? I like bras that hook at the front."

"Not this one, but if we talk again, I'll be sure to have one that hooks in the front. Maybe a black one next time."

Again Austin sighed, "Yes. A black satiny one that hooks in the front. Have you got your bra off yet?"

Betsy made a decision. "I can't quite manage it so I have to put the phone down to take it off. Will you wait for me?"

"Of course."

Betsy put the phone on the bed and pulled her sweatshirt over her head and removed her beige cotton bra. Being clothed felt like a cheat now. Her breasts were small and tight, but at least she was naked from the waist up. She picked up the receiver. "That's so much better. My tits felt like I was being strangled in that tight bra. Now these large white globes are free. Would you like to touch them?"

"Oh God, yes," Austin said, the pitch of his voice rising.

"Close your eyes and reach out your two hands, palms up. I'll lean over and fill your hands with my boobs." She paused, then continued, "Can you feel them in your hands?"

"Oh yes," he said, his voice tight.

"What else would you like to touch? Or would you like me to touch you?" *Can I pull this off?* Betsy wondered. *Touching yet not touching is really weird, but he seems to be enjoying it.*

"I'd like to take my shirt off. Would you rub your boobs on my chest?"

"Of course. Let me help you with your shirt. I'm holding

the front of your shirt and pulling it over your head. Is it all the way off now?"

"Yes."

"Good. Are you naked from the waist up now?"

"Yes."

She wanted to describe touching his chest, but she had no idea whether he was hairy or smooth. Her mind thrashed, trying to think how she could find out. "I want to rub my hands over your chest. How would that feel? Touch your chest and tell me."

"I don't know. Smooth, I guess."

"Yes, so smooth and warm. You feel almost hot. I love the way my hands slide over your skin. Would you touch me while I stroke you?" She stopped, then said, "My breasts are so heavy and feel so . . ." She fumbled for a word. "Satiny. Look at your dark hands on my white skin. That's so sexy it makes me hot. You've got great hands, you know."

"Yeah," he said.

"Now kiss me, lover. Press my hot lips against yours. I'll slide my tongue into your mouth and press my tits against your naked chest. Mmm. I'm moving my body so my nipples rub against you while we kiss. They're getting really hard. You're so sexy."

Betsy turned out the light and stretched out on the bed. She slipped her free hand over her ribs, touching her skin and trying to describe what she was feeling. "I can feel your hard ribs beneath your skin, steel beneath smooth silk." She touched her lips. "Your lips are so soft and warm. Let me touch your tongue with mine."

She heard a long-drawn-out moan and knew she was doing fine so far. "I'm getting hot for you, Austin. Maybe I'll just step back and slide my shorts off." She wiggled out of her sweatpants and bikinis. "I'm naked now. Will you get naked for me?"

"Well, sure." She heard rustling and she assumed Austin was taking off his jeans.

"Are you naked now, baby? I want to see your gorgeous body."

"I'm not so gorgeous, you know," Austin said in a small voice.

"You're gorgeous to me because you're mine right now. Is your cock all hard?"

"Oh yes."

"Touch it and pretend that it's my hand. I'm touching your cock with one hand, wrapping my fingers around the hard shaft. Goodness," she said, "it's so big I can barely close my fingers around you, and it's so hard."

"Yes, it is. I wish I were touching you."

"If you were, here's what you'd feel. My pussy's covered with dark, crispy hair and if you weave your fingers through it, you can find out that I'm wet and hot for you. My cunt is steaming, waiting for your fingers. Rub me, baby. Rub my clit. Like that." Betsy rubbed her now-swollen clit with her finger, amazed at how hot the entire scene was making her. "You make me so hungry. I'm touching my pussy, dreaming that these are your fingertips. I'm sliding my hand farther back so I can slide my index finger into my cunt. Are you holding your cock? Rubbing it?"

"Oh God, yes."

"Get some baby oil so you can rub it faster while I push my finger into my pussy." She waited a beat, then said, "Now two fingers." She actually inserted two fingers into herself, loving the way it felt to be filled.

"God, Mona, you're making me so hot, I can't stand it."

"Oh, love, hold your cock in one hand and stroke it with the other. Pretend they are my hands, with long fingernails that I can use to scratch your skin." All the sexy women had long fingernails, didn't they? "Are you rubbing? Do more.

Make it feel *sooo* good. I'm rubbing myself and making my pussy feel so wonderful."

For a few moments, the phone line was silent as the two touched themselves. "Are you close, Austin?"

"Yes," Austin said, almost breathless.

"Me too," Betsy said, realizing that it was true. She removed her hand, thinking of Larry sitting in the living room. She'd have a surprise for him in a few minutes.

"I'm gonna come, Mona. Right here. You're making me come."

"Yes, my hands are so talented. Close your eyes now, baby," Betsy said. "Picture my mouth approaching the tip of your cock. Shall I suck it?" She made a few slurping sounds. Then Betsy heard a few gasps and an, "Oh, shit."

"You made me come. Just like that, you made me come."

Betsy was dumbfounded. She had actually made Austin climax. Phone sex. This was dynamite. "Was it good, lover?"

"Oh yes. I'm going to use that towel from the floor to clean myself up. I've got to go now. Can I call again next week?"

Holy shit, she thought. He wants to call again. He wants to spend real money next week. "Sure, baby. Mona will be here waiting for you."

"Bye for now," he said, still breathless.

"Bye." She flipped on the light. It was after eight-thirty. She'd been on the phone with him for almost forty minutes. She looked at the small piece of paper with Austin's phone number and the notes she had made. She added smooth chest, hard cock, and the word *suck,* which she assumed was what drove him over the edge. She'd be better prepared next time. She put the paper into her bedtable drawer.

She fumbled in her closet and pulled out an old peignoir, one she hadn't worn since before Phillip was born. She walked down the hall and glanced into the boys' rooms. All three were sound asleep.

She crept down the stairs and found Larry in the living room. "Wow, you look great. How did it go?"

"It was a blast," Betsy said. "Great money, and it's got fringe benefits." She knelt between Larry's knees and unzipped his fly, feeling him get instantly hard.

"What's this?"

"What does it look like?" She reached into the opening and pulled out Larry's erection, already rock-hard.

"It looks like some other guy made you hot."

Betsy looked into her husband's eyes. "I made me hot, and I want you. No one else. Just you." She rubbed the end of Larry's cock over her closed lips, feeling the slippery fluid already leaking out. "Want me?"

"You know it," Larry moaned. "I kept thinking about some guy getting his rocks off while you talked to him. It drove me crazy."

"It made me hot knowing he was coming, but he's not here. He's just a voice. On the other hand, you are here, now. And I want you." She kissed the tip of Larry's cock.

"You really got off on it."

"I did, and I want to take it out on you." She stood up, opened her robe and climbed onto the sofa on her knees, straddling Larry's lap. With little preliminary, she lowered her steaming cunt on his hard shaft. Using her thigh muscles, she raised and lowered her body, fucking his cock without his having to move.

It took no more than a few moments for him to come, spurting semen deep inside of her. Then he took his fingers and rubbed Betsy's clit until she came, the spasms rocking her entire body.

Silently, they cleaned themselves up, closed up the downstairs, and went up to the bedroom. Quickly they readied themselves for bed and, both naked, climbed between the sheets. "If anything about this bothers you, I won't do it again," Betsy said, prepared to give it all up if Larry wanted her to.

Larry thought about it for a minute, then said, "I was really jealous as I sat downstairs and thought about you on the phone with some other guy, but what followed was terrific. You're right. It doesn't matter how you get hot, as long as you work off your heat with me and no one else. I'm not ready to share your body."

"I have no intention of sharing my body with anyone but you." She slipped her arms around her husband's waist. "He wants to call me again next week, this time for real money."

"No shit. You must be good at it. What did you say?"

"You know," Betsy said, her tone serious, "somehow that's private and I don't think it feels right to tell you. But anytime you want me to talk dirty to you, I'll be delighted. You will, of course, have to pay." Betsy grabbed her husband's already hardening cock. "I know just how."

"Well," Betsy said to Alice, "Larry and I didn't get to sleep for quite a while." A wide grin split her face.

"That's amazing," Alice said. "I guess I'm not surprised, though. You were always good at everything you put your mind to."

"I don't know about everything, but I have more customers than I can handle, so to speak. I spend only one night a week on the phone, and can only take three or four calls."

"Have you ever seen any of these guys?"

"Nope. I wouldn't know them if they bumped into me in the food court. It's great that way. Anonymous. We can each imagine anything we want."

"Larry still isn't jealous?"

"Occasionally he needs reassurance, but I love him to pieces and in his heart he knows there's no danger at all."

At that moment Phillip and Brandon ran out of the arcade. "Mom," Phillip said, "can we have another dollar each? Please? You can take it out of our allowances."

"Please, Mom," Brandon chimed in. "We still have ten minutes. Please?"

"Let me," Alice said. She fished her wallet out of her pocketbook and gave the boys each a dollar.

"What do you say?" Betsy said as the boys darted off.

"Thanks, Alice," they said in unison, then headed back into the arcade.

"The boys think you're in phone sales. Don't you worry that they will find out?"

"Not really. It might happen, but we are careful. They know that Mom disappears every Tuesday evening into a room behind a locked door. It's the only time doors are locked in our house, so they know it's important. Most of the time, Larry takes them out for dinner and a movie so I have more privacy. It really works out fine since Larry and the boys get to spend quality time together each week. He helps them with homework, then puts them to bed while I'm locked in the den. I paid for that room, you know. With my earnings."

"If you do so well, why do you continue at Dr. Tannenbaum's office?"

"I like the work and with three boys to put through college, every cent is important."

"If you don't mind me asking, how much do you make?"

"Velvet charges $2.99 per minute and I get half."

Alice did some quick calculations. "That's ninety dollars an hour."

"Not many calls last an hour, but yes, that's what it adds up to."

"Wow."

"Yes, wow. You could do it too."

Alice barked a laugh. "I could not."

"Of course you could. You're a great storyteller and that has to mean you've got a great imagination. Just think about it. It would solve all your money problems. I can introduce you to Velvet and you can discuss it, no commitment."

"I don't think so."

"Why not?"

"Because."

"Good answer." Betsy glanced at her watch. "It's almost eight and Larry will think I've absconded with the boys." She took the last few gulps of her coffee. "Nah. He knows that if I ever abscond, I'll leave the boys here so I can have a little quiet." She stood up, tossed her cappuccino cup in the trash and picked up her pocketbook. "I'm going to find my two darlings, then get Josh and get out of here. Alice, think about what I told you and I'll see you at work tomorrow."

"Hmm," Alice said. "You know, I'll think about it."

Chapter 3

Alice watched Betsy stride into the arcade and emerge minutes later with her two protesting boys. The three turned and waved. Weakly, Alice waved back, shaking her head. Betsy. A phone-sex person. *I wonder what you call them,* she thought. *Phone sluts?* Betsy was not a slut. She was the nicest human being Alice had ever met. But this?

Alice stared unseeingly at the front of the arcade. *What's wrong with phone sex? She never meets the guys she talks with. She's never been unfaithful to Larry and Larry knows all about it. If he doesn't mind, why should I?* She shook her head again. *Now she wants me to do it too. Ridiculous.*

Alice sipped the cold remains of her cappuccino, then stood and dropped the cup into the trash. Phone sex. Me? Not a chance. But half of $2.99 a minute. Ninety dollars an hour. With just an hour or two, she could manage to have her mother stay at Rutlandt. Could she do it? She shook her head. Not a chance.

Slowly, Alice wandered the mall, gazing into store windows, not really seeing any of the items. Her mind was whirling, both with Betsy's revelation and with the idea that she could make some real money that way. *Even if I could,* she said to herself, *who knows whether I'd be good at it. Good enough to attract regular customers. Could I talk about sex? What the hell do I know about good sex. Ralph wasn't worth much in the bedroom.*

She pictured her ex-husband, paunchy and dull, and over fifty now. *I still have no clue what ever possessed me.* Although Alice hadn't been pretty, Ralph Finch, a longtime family friend, had watched her change from girl to woman and had wanted her. As he told her, he found her innocence appealing, her intelligence fascinating, and her sense of humor delightful. He had little chance to meet and get to know women with his job as a long-haul truck driver so he had never married. Now it was time to have a wife and start a family and what could be better than someone he already knew well. Love? Passion? They would grow in time.

Her parents had been delighted with the idea and Alice really liked "Uncle Ralph." So, the day after Alice's high school graduation, they were married in the living room of the Waterman home.

The marriage was a bore. Alice worked as the receptionist for an obstetrician while Ralph drove his long-haul truck. They were apart for long periods of time and slowly Alice realized that she was happier when Ralph was not around. When he came home, he enjoyed watching TV, eating the massive amounts of food that Alice cooked to fill him up, sex, and not much else.

Evenings, with Alice beside him on the sofa, they watched sitcoms. As the evening progressed, Ralph would drape his arm around Alice's shoulder and fondle her breast. Then he took her hand and put it on his crotch. "It's been a long time, girl. See how ready I am?"

Usually Alice wasn't nearly ready but, feeling it was her job to satisfy her husband, she allowed Ralph to lead her into the bedroom. She undressed and, after coating his cock with K-Y Jelly, he pushed it into her. "I'll never understand why you don't get wet," he said during almost every session. "Maybe you should ask that doctor you work for."

She asked and was told that everything about her physiology was normal. "You might suggest that your husband take his time," the doctor had recommended. She hadn't mentioned that to Ralph.

After almost three years of marriage, Ralph arrived home one day from two weeks on the road. He set his suitcase beside the door and walked slowly into the bedroom, with Alice following. "Honey, I'm really sorry about this, but I'm leaving. There's someone else."

"What?" Alice had been completely unaware that he had any problem with their marriage. She dropped onto the edge of the bed and grabbed a tissue from the box on the bedside table.

"In L.A.," Ralph continued. "She's my age and hot to trot. She loves to do all the things that you don't. She loves *The Cosby Show* and *Golden Girls* and she's great in the sack, if you know what I mean. You just never seem to enjoy it." Alice merely stared, unable to get a word in edgewise, even if she'd had anything to say. "Anyway," Ralph said, "we've been seeing each other each time I drive to the coast. Her grown son just moved out and she wants me to move in with her. I'm gonna do it." As Alice stared, Ralph began to throw the rest of his clothes into their only other large suitcase. "You need someone younger anyway. You need to have some fun."

"I need?" Alice choked past her thick throat.

"Sure. You need a young stud. I know you're not happy."

"What do you care about what I need? This has nothing

to do with me. You've found someone better." She hovered between anger and panic.

"Listen. I'm not saying this real well, but it's for the best for both of us." He pulled something from his back pocket. "I went to the bank and took a thousand dollars from our savings account. Here's the passbook." He handed her the slim leather book. "There's almost seven hundred dollars left. Use it to get a divorce. I won't contest anything."

"I put most of that money in there," Alice shrieked. "How dare you take that money so you can move in with that, that woman."

Ralph tossed his few remaining shirts and sweaters into the suitcase. "I've got a load outside and it's going to L.A. I'm not coming back."

"What about the apartment? What about my family?"

"Your job will cover the rent and I really don't care about your family."

"My dad's your best friend. At least call him and explain."

"No time. You tell him whatever you want. Tell him I'll write from the coast."

"Don't bother."

Alice had cried for several days, then she had gotten along surprisingly well. Their first Christmas apart, Ralph had sent her a card with a picture of a decorated tree standing in the middle of a beach. He'd signed the card Ralph and Missy. Alice had dropped it into the garbage. Her parents had been supportive and as helpful as they could be and life quickly took on a new character.

She worked, dated occasionally, and spent increasing amounts of time with Betsy and her family. She felt as close to Larry and the boys as she did to her own family. They had all stood beside her at her father's funeral, celebrated at her sister's wedding, and they spent every holiday together. Now she realized that she hadn't known them. Not by a long shot.

Alice wandered aimlessly around the mall and found herself in front of Victoria's Secret. She gazed in the window at a display of bra and panty sets in vibrant jewel tones. *Sure. Me. Think like a sexpot. Right. Never happen. But the money would be so nice.*

She drove home on automatic pilot, her mind still reeling from Betsy's revelations. As the door to her apartment closed behind her, Alice leaned down to scratch Roger, her brown tabby cat, behind his ears. Always noisy, Roger *merrowed* and rubbed his sides along her legs. "And hello to you," she said. "You'll never believe what I found out today."

Merrow.

She picked up Roger and settled on the sofa with him on her lap. She told the cat everything that Betsy had confessed to her. When he *merrowed* again, Alice said, "Right. I know. You're surprised too."

The ringing of the phone startled them both. Roger dug his claws into Alice's thighs and darted into the bedroom. *No one ever calls me this late.* Worried that it might be her sister with bad news about her mother, she answered, "Hello?"

It was Betsy's voice. "I thought I'd call and make sure you're not shocked or mad at me or something. You don't hate me?"

"Betsy, you know I don't hate you and I'm not mad. Shocked, maybe a little, and maybe just a bit sad that you didn't tell me sooner."

"I didn't know how you'd take it all. You always were a bit . . ."

"A bit what?"

"Sorry. That didn't come out right. Listen. Let me say it this way. Everyone in the world except me, and maybe Larry, thinks that you're a bit of a prude. I know that beneath that straight exterior, there's someone who's willing and able to give the sexy side of life a try."

"A prude? People think I'm a prude?" She slumped back on the overstuffed tan sofa, the one on which Ralph used to watch TV.

"People who don't know you like I do might think you were, well, the old-fashioned spinster type. But you're not, and I know it."

"Spinster type?" Roger jumped onto Alice's lap and she began to scratch him behind his ears. She looked down. Cat, well-worn tan sofa, empty house. Spinster type.

"I wouldn't butt into your life for anything, and you know that. It just seems to me that you've stopped living before you ever started." When Alice gasped, Betsy continued, "Now don't get all defensive and just listen for a moment. I never meant to start this, but maybe it's time I did. After Ralph left, you closed yourself off. You shut everything that was womanly away. You work, hang out with us, and you know we love you, but you need a social life."

"You mean a man."

"Or men, yes. That's what I mean. Have you ever had good sex? I remember Ralph, and I doubt it. I know what's under all that bullshit you've built around yourself. I remember the hours we used to talk about boys. You had wants and needs back then. You used to fantasize about Ponch and John on *CHiPs,* just like the rest of us. Remember those cruises we used to plan on *The Love Boat?* You got Gopher and I got, oh, what was the name of the cute guy who took the pictures?"

Alice chuckled and put her feet up on the coffee table. "Ace. He was only there at the end. I do remember. We used to spend long evenings talking when we were supposed to be doing social studies."

"So what happened to her?"

"Who?"

"The you who used to be so alive?"

Alice was silent. She'd never heard Betsy talk this way. "I like my life."

"Spending time with my kids? I have never pushed you and I'm not going to start now. I do want you to think about all this, though, and consider that this job, if it works out, may be a way to find your sexual self without any risk. It's just the phone."

"If I'm such a spinster type," she said, bitterly, "why the hell do you think I'd be any good at this phone stuff?"

"Because I know you better than you know yourself. There's a real woman under there, with hot erotic fantasies and dreams. This would be the perfect outlet. You're a natural storyteller. Even the boys know that. You could use that talent and create erotic fantasies for nice, frustrated men who just want someone to talk dirty with."

Alice tried to keep the pain out of her voice. "I really don't think so but I understand all this a bit better now."

"Alice, don't be hurt. You know how much I care about you. I love you like a sister. Please, think over all I've said and I'll see you in the morning."

The morning. How would she face her friend? She'd have to. If she lost Betsy, who did she have? She gazed at the blank TV screen. Wasn't that the point Betsy was trying to make? "Yeah. I'll see you in the morning. Night."

"Night, babe." The phone went silent in her hand. Slowly she replaced the receiver on the base, picked up the cat, and walked slowly into the bedroom, turning off lights as she went. She flipped on the bedroom light and looked around. The room was pretty much unchanged from the day that Ralph left, nearly ten years earlier. Actually from long before that since Alice had moved into Ralph's apartment after they were married. She looked around. Heavy wooden furniture that had been Ralph's. Faded blue bedspread and blue denim drapes that she had made from an old sheet their first winter together. Dull gray carpet with a nail-polish stain beside the bed. It was pretty dismal but she seldom really saw it.

Mindlessly Alice turned on the TV, already tuned to *Headline News.* "God, Roger," she said, dropping onto the bed still holding the cat, "maybe Betsy's right. *Headline News.* It's nine-thirty and I'm watching *Headline News.* If it were Tuesday, Betsy would be on the phone to God-knows-who talking about God-knows-what." She scratched the cat under his chin. "You're the only man in my life. Prude. Spinster type. Shit."

Throughout the night, Alice tossed and turned, unable to get her conversations with Betsy out of her mind. The following morning, feeling cranky from lack of sleep, she arrived at Dr. Tannenbaum's office. Betsy was already there dressed in a light purple scrub top and matching pants, her brown hair pulled back with two gold barrettes. "Morning," Betsy said, sounding disgustingly cheerful. "You look like shit."

"I didn't get much sleep." Alice pulled off her coat, revealing a cartoon character–print scrub top and jeans. She wore only lipstick and there were faint purple circles underneath her eyes.

"I was afraid of that." Betsy took Alice's coat, hung it up then hugged her friend. "I'm sorry. I replayed the discussions we had. My diatribe, actually, and I'm afraid lots of it didn't come out quite the way I intended."

Alice hugged Betsy then stepped back. "You know, I thought it all through, too, and I have to admit that lots of what you said made sense." She smiled. "I hate it when you're right."

"Right how?" Betsy's expression was wary.

"I do need a life. I'm not sure whether I need the one you're offering, but it's certainly worth a bit more thought and I really do need the money."

The two women walked into the reception room and sat

down. "I'm really sorry for a lot of what I said," Betsy said.

"It's the way you feel."

"Yes, but I don't want to push you. You don't have to do anything you don't want to do. If you want to talk more about it, let me know, but I promise that I won't mention it again."

"You won't have to. I'll wager I won't be able to think about anything else." The door opened and the two women looked up. "Good morning, Mrs. McAllister," Alice said to the morning's first patient. "How's your lovely new grand baby?"

Over the next few days Alice spent a great deal of time talking to her sister. Her mother's condition had stabilized and even improved a bit and Sue's friend was working out well as a daytime caregiver. They had applied to Rutlandt and two or three second-best nursing homes, hoping for admission by May first. If Rutlandt came through, they'd have to figure out how to pay for it, or turn it down in favor of the less-expensive place.

The following Tuesday evening, Alice sat in her living room, holding Roger and trying to picture Betsy on the phone with her customers. *Where would I even start? I can't talk dirty. I'm not even sure what guys like. I certainly didn't know what Ralph liked. Guys like women who know how to perform oral sex. Ralph used to joke about it. "Too bad you don't give head, girl," he used to tell her. Why didn't he ever let me try?*

Since Dr. Tannenbaum's office was closed on Wednesdays, Alice ran a few errands in the neighborhood, but continued to dwell on Betsy's phone business. Bizarre pictures whirled in her head. Betsy with shiny flame-red lipstick, her pursed lips near the receiver. Men with no faces but large ears, listening, talking, touching themselves. There were moments when she thought she might be able to do what her best friend did, but there were hours when she knew she couldn't.

Thursday morning, Alice arrived at work before Betsy and expectantly waited for her friend. "Morning," Betsy said, breezing in despite a freezing March drizzle that had soaked Alice's coat and made driving hazardous.

"How'd it go Tuesday evening?" Alice asked, watching Betsy hang up her heavy coat. "I kept thinking about you."

"It went great. It almost always does."

"Almost always?"

"Oh, occasionally it's difficult to get on the same wavelength with someone new," she said, walking into the empty reception area. "You have to use some charm and skill to find out what turns them on."

"How did you learn all that?" Alice asked, feeling more daunted than ever.

"Time, and lots of calls. And Velvet's a great help. She's been doing this for almost fifteen years and she knows all the tricks."

"Where do you start? I mean how do you know what will turn someone on?"

"I get lots of those shrink-wrapped magazines and read them from cover to cover. I particularly read the stories and the ads for phone sex. You'd be amazed what you can learn from what the publishers of those magazines think men like. I assume they're right since the magazines sell."

"I could do that, but I'd feel like a fool going into a store and buying *Penthouse* or *Playboy*."

"Why? Nice folks read them, you know. Now, of course, there's the Internet. You can find thousands of stories out there. I browse occasionally for new ideas and, along with the pictures of naked men and women, there are lots of pieces of good, erotic fiction out there." Maureen, the dental hygienist, walked in and hung up her coat. After the usual good mornings, she walked into the operatory area and the two women lowered their voices.

"That's a good idea. Maybe I'll do that and see whether I could say some of that stuff."

"You know, Velvet has a large number of guys who phone regularly. I wonder whether anyone likes the reticent, shy type who'll say the naughty words only reluctantly." Betsy's eyes glazed over momentarily. "That might be appealing actually."

"Really?"

"I don't know. Look, if you think you want to do this, I'll give Velvet a call and ask. I'd want you to meet her anyway."

That night, Alice signed on to her Internet account and went searching. She found several stories that seemed like they might be good so she printed them out. When she was done, she went into the bedroom with a beer. Roger curled up beside her as she started to read.

WITHOUT A WORD
by Silent Sal

Michelle lay somewhere between sleep and wakefulness, listening to the upstairs neighbors stomp around their bedroom getting ready for bed. She glanced at the clock. Almost 2:00 A.M. *I shouldn't get too angry since it happens so seldom,* she told herself. *They're such nice people, they probably just aren't thinking.*

She felt her husband, Bill, scramble out of his side of the bed and wander to the bathroom. The door closed, the light went on, and then later it went out again. In a few minutes he was back in the warm cocoon and, with a yawn, Michelle leisurely climbed out of her side and padded to the bathroom.

Several minutes later, slightly chilled from the cold night air, she climbed back under the thick quilt, thinking how glad she was that unlike Bill, she could go to the john in the middle of the night without having to turn on the light. As she snuggled her chest against Bill's large, warm back, she had a few fleeting erotic flashes. Well, she reasoned, if she fell back to sleep, she'd awake refreshed.

Wait a moment, she told herself. *Why should I go back to sleep? I have the desire and Bill's right here. Why not do something about it?*

She had never been particularly bold about lovemaking, leaving most of the first moves to her husband. Bill was almost always the initiator of sex, but why shouldn't she be the aggressor from time to time? She cuddled more tightly against his back and felt her nipples harden in response to her wandering thoughts. Was he still awake? She'd find out quickly enough.

She stroked Bill's arm, just enjoying the feel of the short, wiry hairs that covered his skin. She seldom took the time to enjoy touching her husband so she spent several minutes stroking his arm, hands, and fingers. Then she reached around and flattened her palms on Bill's chest and stroked the smooth surface. When her palms contacted Bill's small nipples, she rubbed them, then used a short fingernail to scratch the tiny nub into life. Amazed, she felt it harden beneath her finger. She wiggled her hips so her pubic bone rubbed against Bill's tailbone and realized that she was getting wetter. Bill hadn't said anything or reacted in any obvious way, but Michelle became aware of a slight hoarseness to his breathing. *He's awake all right. He's playing possum so I'll continue, so he must be enjoying what I'm doing.*

She slid her palm down to Bill's waist and felt his abdominal muscles contract. With her cheek against his back, she could hear and feel his breathing quicken. When he tried to turn over, she held on, enjoying her position behind him. Slowly Michelle slid her palm down his belly and suddenly his cock, hard and throbbing, bumped against the back of her hand. Seemingly content now to remain on his side with his wife in charge, Bill gasped and lay still.

He's so horny, she thought, *and I did that.* It was a revelation. She knew in her mind that he would enjoy it if she took the lead occasionally, but she had always been hesitant. *What if I do it wrong or he thinks I'm being silly or he's not in the mood?* Worried, in the past, when she had considered making the first move, she had demurred. *Well,* she thought, *he is obviously enjoying this. Maybe I can do it more often.* She quieted her thoughts and concentrated on the feel of Bill's body. As her palm caressed his belly, the back of her hand caressed his hard cock.

She kissed his back and licked a wide stripe. Then, unable to get enough of his skin into her mouth to nip him, she scraped her teeth along his spine. She knew full well that he wanted her to grasp his cock, but she resisted the urge, teasing him. She knew that he wouldn't ask, leaving her to set the pace, unwilling to disturb the mood. He was enjoying the silence, the dark, the slight mystery and anonymity of it all as much as she was.

Michelle squirmed, feeling Bill's skin against her now-heated body. Her belly against his back, her thighs against his ass cheeks, her breasts against his shoulder blades, she moved like a cat in heat. God, he felt so good.

Then she did it. She grasped Bill's cock and held it tightly. She had held his cock many times before, to guide it into her waiting body, but she'd never actually rubbed it to climax. Could she do it? She wanted him inside of her, but this was too intriguing to resist. Although it was scary, she wanted to try. She held him tightly and felt his whole body tense. Her entire body was in tune with his and she was aware of his every reaction to what she was doing. She held fast, pulling her hand upward toward the tip of his erection. The end was already wet with his pre-come and she used the tip of her index finger to rub the lubricant around the head of his penis.

As she did so, she felt his body tighten still more and his hips moved almost involuntarily. *God, this is so good,* she thought again. She squeezed again and pulled her hand downward toward the base of the hard rod, using his body's own lubricant to ease her way. Again to the tip and more fluid.

Soon his cock was slippery and she could slide her hand up and down in a slow rhythm. Feeling braver, she stopped and decided to explore a bit. She slid one finger up and down the underside of Bill's cock, then slid farther down and touched his balls. The moan she heard and felt was all the reassurance she needed. It was a bit difficult to reach, but she ran the pad of her finger over the surface of his sac. Did she want him to turn over so she could do more? No, she realized. If he lay on his back she'd be tempted to climb on top of him and she really wanted to see whether she could bring him to climax without intercourse.

She returned her attention to his cock and stroked, first toward the tip, then downward to the base. She heard air hiss out between Bill's teeth. His cock took on a life of its own and moved beneath her hand. Bill sighed, then groaned softly.

Michelle flattened her hand on the underside of his cock, pressed it against his abdomen and rubbed. She felt him pulse, then his hips jerked and his cock twitched against her palm. He came, silently, his entire body throbbing against her. Her hand was now covered with his sticky come and some of it dripped onto the sheet. Wordlessly, Bill grabbed a corner of the top sheet and wiped the goo from her hand and his abdomen.

Still silent, he turned and pushed her onto her back. His mouth found her hard, erect nipple, and his teeth caused shards of pleasure to rocket through her already aroused body. His mouth alternated between her nipples until she was almost crying with need. Unwilling to break the silence, she pushed against Bill's shoulders, urging him to use his hands to finish her off. She heard a slight chuckle, then he slithered down beneath the covers and locked his mouth on her now-needy pussy. His tongue flicked over her clit, then lapped up the fluids that had collected between her swollen inner lips.

Now almost crazy with lust, Michelle tangled her long fingers in her husband's curly hair and held his face tightly against her need. A finger pushed inside her channel and, as he licked, he drove first one then two fingers in and out of her hot pussy. Her belly clenched and her legs trembled. It was only moments before she came, spasms echoing through her body as flaming colors flashed behind her eyes. Almost unable to catch her breath, she gently pushed Bill's face aside and he slid up and cuddled against her. In almost no time, they were both back to sleep.

In the morning, Michelle awoke to find Bill propped on his elbow, watching her. "I had the most wonderful dream," he purred.

"You did?" she said, a grin spreading across her face.

He leaned over until she could feel his warm breath on her face. "I dreamed that a sexy woman held me and stroked me in the middle of the night until I came. She didn't say anything, but I could have sworn it was you."

"I had a wonderful dream too. Some sexy man used his very talented mouth to make me come."

"Hmm. Matching dreams. I wonder whether that has some significance?"

"I think it does. I certainly think so."

Alice put the pages beside her on the bed and lifted Roger onto her lap. That woman had had her doubts too. She hadn't been sure how to touch her husband, but she had done what felt good to both of them. Why hadn't she ever done anything like that? Her sex life had been a bust and she hadn't done anything to make it better. She hadn't known anything, but how was she supposed to have learned? Ralph had never told her what to do, never even suggested. She had been a failure as a wife, but didn't Ralph bear any of the responsibility? Wasn't it his job, if only a little, to help her, teach her? She had read several sex books their first year together and had tried to talk to her husband about their love life but he had always put her off. "Oh, girl, it's all right. I'm happy with things the way they are." But she hadn't been happy and she knew now that he hadn't been happy either.

So whose fault was it? Was she a prude who would never be any good at sex? No, and it wasn't her fault, nor was it Ralph's. And what about her life since? Hadn't she just given up? After Ralph left, she had her job, her family, and Betsy. Was that normal? She hadn't really dated, and she hadn't had anything resembling sex in what seemed like forever.

She sighed and said, "Roger, where am I now? Thirty-two years old. A spinster type who's never even lived." She dumped Roger onto the bed and strode into the bathroom. She closed the door and looked at herself in the full-length mirror. "Dumpy," she said. Face? Plain. She tucked her shirt into her jeans, sucked in her stomach and pulled a large gulp of air into her lungs. Figure? Ordinary. Overweight. Boobs? Average. Quickly she stripped off her clothes and looked at her naked body. "Underneath all those clothes there's nothing good." Thighs? Heavy. Belly? Rounded and getting rounder. Tits? Sagging. She lifted her arms, looked at the slight droop beneath her upper arms and sighed. She wandered back into the bedroom and pulled on the oversized New York Jets T-shirt she slept in. "You know, Roger, it's only phone sex. They'd never see me. I could look like a hippo for all anyone would know, and I could become anyone."

She crouched beside her bookshelf and found the collection of how-to sex books she had bought while she was married. She pulled one out and stared at the dust. *I could learn a lot. I remember that these had a lot of good ideas. I could do some reading and learn.* "I really could, Roger."

She climbed into bed and picked up the second set of pages she had printed from the Internet. One more before sleep. Maybe it would lead to good dreams.

Chapter 4

In the Hot Tub

It had been a terrible week for twenty-eight-year-old Eric La Monte. First, he and his girlfriend of almost a year had split. "I want some freedom," she had said, "some time to explore who I really am." Eric had sat on his side of the bed in their Palm Springs condo and watched her pack. Then he'd spent three days explaining her absence to his entire family and all his friends. Why? everyone asked. God only knows, became his litany. Finally, on Thursday, his district manager had arrived for a three-day surprise visit to the supermarket he managed. Sure, he thought later, everything could have been a lot worse on that front. He'd received only a few "needs improvement" warnings, but, all in all, it had been an awful week.

Now it was Saturday evening, and he was exhausted and alone. He lay on the bed and tried to sleep, but it was impossible. Every time he closed his eyes he thought about Marge or Mr. Pomerantz. Neither mental picture was geared to allow him to sleep. "Shit," he muttered climbing out of bed as the red numerals on the clock read 1:07 A.M. "I gotta relax." Although it was early summer, it was still over eighty degrees. The condo's hot tub and pool closed at eleven but he could easily climb the fence and lounge in the hot bubbling water for a while. "It'll help me unwind."

With just a towel around his loins, Eric walked to the fence around the pool, surprised to find the gate unlocked. Most of the lights were out, so he heard rather than saw that the bubbles were on in the tub. Through the mist, he saw a woman's gray head. Since much of Palm Springs's population was made up of retirees, Eric assumed that the person in the pool was some ancient specimen boiling the arthritis out of old bones at 1:00 A.M. "Shit," he muttered again. "Some old bitch is where I want to be." He remembered that, since he had assumed he'd be alone, he had not worn a bathing suit. "Fuck her," he hissed, striding to the edge of the tub, dropping the towel and climbing into the bubbling cauldron.

As he settled into the hot water, Eric looked through the dimly lighted mist at the woman sitting across the pool. She was not bad-looking, maybe only fifty or so, with flushed cheeks and wet, shoulder-length hair. Eric ignored her, cradled his head on the concrete rim, draped his arms over the edge, and closed his eyes.

"I thought I'd be the only one here at this hour," her soft voice said over the bubble noise. "I'm Carol."

"Eric," he grunted.

"Well," Carol said, "it's going to get a bit embarrassing in here in a minute or so. The timer on the pump has only a short while to go and I'm afraid I'm not wearing anything either. I usually reset the dial for a second go-around."

"No sweat," Eric said. "I promise I won't look if you want to extend the time."

"Thanks." Eric could hear the smile in her voice. Then

he heard her leave the water and quietly pad over to the controls. He heard the creak of the dials. He couldn't resist, so he opened his eyes and looked. Not bad, he thought. Not bad at all. She was slender and firm, with a slight droop to her bosom but in general not bad. Not Marge, of course but . . .

She padded back to the steps and slowly walked down into the heated water. "You're looking," she said, seeming unperturbed.

Eric slammed his eyes shut. "Sorry," he mumbled.

"I'm not," she said. "I like it when men look at me."

Eric opened his eyes again and saw that she was still standing, thigh-deep in the warm water. "You're not bad to look at," he said.

He watched as she slowly took a handful of heated water and released it over her right breast. Then another over her left. "I love the heat," she said.

Despite the debilitating effect of the hot water, Eric felt a stirring in his groin. "How come you're here after hours?" he asked, deflecting the conversation before his cock got embarrassingly hard.

"I couldn't sleep. I often come out here after midnight so I got a key from a particularly friendly security guard."

The way she said *particularly friendly* had Eric's ears perked. How friendly, he wondered.

"How about you?" she asked, lowering herself into the water beside him. "How come you're here tonight?"

"Couldn't sleep either," Eric said. He could sense her presence beside him although he couldn't actually feel her skin.

"I couldn't help but notice that Marge moved out."

"What do you know about that?"

"There's not much real privacy here. I hope it was your idea. Breakups can be so difficult."

"Actually it was hers," Eric said, closing his eyes. "I don't really want to talk about it." Suddenly Eric felt a hand on his leg.

"I'm sure you don't, Eric," Carol said. "It's tough."

The hand was kneading his thigh. It could be just a gesture of sympathy, he told himself, but it was having an effect on his cock anyway. *I've got to change the subject before I say something dumb.* "Are you married?" Was that a change of topic?

"Used to be, but we were divorced almost five years ago."

"That's tough," Eric said.

"Not really," Carol said, her hand still kneading the flesh of Eric's thigh. "I make do."

This is getting to be a bit too much, Eric thought. *She can't be doing what I think she's doing. This sort of thing doesn't happen. Not to me.* "Oh." Eric squeezed his eyes shut, trying to ignore the hand on his thigh. "Which unit is yours?" he asked.

"I'm in B-204. It's quite comfortable for just me."

The hand crept a bit higher, the fingers almost in his groin. "I'll bet it is," he croaked.

He felt her mouth close to his cheek. "I hope I'm not upsetting you," she said into his ear. Then she giggled. "Actually I hope I am." The hand found his testicles and one finger brushed the surface. "Am I?"

Eric opened his eyes and looked at the woman sitting next to him. There could be no misinterpreting her movements. She was seducing him. His arm was still on the edge of the pool. He draped it around her shoulders and pulled her closer. "Yes," he said, his mouth against hers, "you are. Is that what you want?"

Carol's tongue reached out and licked the sweat from Eric's upper lip. "Oh yes. I want to bother you a lot."

He kissed her then, pressing his wet mouth against hers, tasting salt and chlorine and her. His mouth opened and his tongue touched hers. So hot, deep, and wet. Her mouth seemed to pull him closer.

His hands found her breasts, soft, full, and floaty in the bubbling water. He had never played with weightless breasts before. They felt loose and incredibly sexy. Then he couldn't concentrate on anything, because her hand had surrounded his cock and now squeezed tightly. "God," she breathed, "you're so big."

She probably says that to everyone, he thought in the small part of his brain still capable of thought. It's such a cliché come-on line, but he went with it all. His cock was the biggest ever, and she wanted it.

He slid his hands to her waist and started to lift her onto his ready staff.

"Not so fast, baby," she purred. "I'm not nearly ready for you yet." She stood up and climbed out of the tub, beckoning him to follow. He was incapable of resistance. She straddled a plastic-webbed lounge chair, one foot on the concrete at either side. She patted the chair between her legs. "Here, baby," she purred and he sat facing her.

She lay back and smiled. "The air is just cool enough to feel good on my hot, wet body. Yours too?"

"Yes," Eric said, his hands scrambling in her crotch. She reached down and held her labia open. "Touch nice and soft right now," she said. "Rub in the folds. I like to be touched everywhere."

Eric had calmed a bit and was now able to think coherently. He slowly explored every crease between Carol's legs. He'd always been too hungry to pay much attention to Marge's body. Now he got to know Carol's. When he rubbed back toward her anus, she moaned and moved her hips. When he brushed her clit, she gasped. It was wonderful. She was telling him so clearly exactly what she wanted, without saying a word.

She was so wet, he noticed. Slippery juice oozed backward

and wet her puckered rear entry. He ran his finger around the opening and Carol trembled. Could he?

"I like what you're doing," she said, as if reading his mind. "You can do anything you like. I'll tell you to stop if I don't like it."

He had never just sat and touched a woman like this before, watching her face and body respond to his fingers. It was arousing, yet as hard as his cock was, he was also capable of waiting, enjoying the now and not rushing forward. He pressed his index finger against her puckered rear hole and marveled at how it slipped in just a bit.

"Oh, God," she hissed. "That's incredible."

Eric slipped the finger in just a bit more and watched Carol writhe. He used his other hand to stroke her clit, knowing that she was close to climax. Part of him wanted to plunge his cock into her, but another part wanted to finish her off just this way. He pulled the finger from her ass, then pushed it back in. Her juices were flowing so copiously that his hand was soaked, his finger wet enough to penetrate her rear hole. Slowly the digit slid farther and farther into her rear passage. Faster and faster he rubbed her hard nub.

When he thought she was ready, he leaned down and placed his mouth over her clit. He flicked his tongue firmly over the hard bud and felt her back arch and her hands tangle in his hair. "Yes, yes," she hissed. "Now."

He felt her come, felt the spasms in her ass, felt her cunt pulse against his mouth. He didn't move until he felt her begin to relax. "I want to fuck you," he said.

"I know," Carol said, panting, "but let's do this my way. Please."

Eric shrugged. He was beyond caring about the "how."

Slowly, Carol got up and moved Eric around so he was sitting properly on the chair, her body stretched out between his legs. "I love it this way," she whispered. Her hands cupped his balls and her mouth found his cock. She licked the tip, then blew on the wet spot. She licked the length of his shaft underneath, then each side. She kneaded his balls, then insinuated one finger beneath his sacs, reaching for his anus.

He closed his eyes. No one had ever touched him there and he wasn't sure he would like it. He did. It was electric. Shafts of pure pleasure rocketed down his cock as the familiar tightness started in his belly and balls. "I'm going to shoot," he said, his voice hoarse.

Carol lifted her head. "Oh yes. Do it, baby. Shoot for me." She took the length of him in her mouth as she rimmed his asshole.

He couldn't hold back and the jism boiled from his loins into her mouth. He opened his eyes and looked at her cheeks as she tried unsuccessfully to swallow his come. Small dribbles escaped from the corners of her mouth and wet his balls.

A few minutes later Carol took her towel, dipped it in the hot tub and tenderly washed Eric's groin. "I have to go in now," she said.

Limp, drained, and unable to move, Eric said, "I wish you'd stay."

"No you don't," she said, smiling. "You need to recover alone. But I'm here almost every night about one o'clock. Come back whenever you get lonely."

"Good night," Eric said. "I know I'll be here again soon."

"Oh," she said, opening the gate, "I hope so."

Eric watched her back and remembered thinking of her as an old bitch. *Gray hair indeed,* he thought. *The fire's still on in that sexy furnace. I'll never underestimate older women again.*

Alice put the pages on the bed-table beside her and flipped off the light. *I'm only thirty-two,* she thought. *I could learn. I really could. Then I'd be like Carol. I just need a little practice.* She yawned and was asleep almost instantly.

In her dream she was in a hot tub, naked. The water bubbled all around her, teasing and tickling. She looked around and all she could see were palm trees, thick and completely surrounding the tub, obliterating any houses and prying eyes. There was a man in the water with her, across the tub, an old man with thick white hair and a wizened face with deep wrinkles and smile lines. "Ralph?" she asked.

"No. He's gone," the man said. "I'm here with you."

"Oh," she said, the bubbles now causing steam to rise from the tub. What was she doing in a hot tub, nude, with some strange man? She moved to cover herself but realized that with all the bubbles, nothing could be seen below the water.

"It's your turn now," he said.

"My turn for what?"

"It's your turn for yourself."

"What does that mean?"

The man shook his head sadly. "If you don't know, well . . . It's really all up to you."

"You talk in riddles," Alice said.

"No, I don't. You don't want to hear."

"Do you mean I can do this? I should do this?"

"Only you know."

She rested her head on the edge of the tub and closed her eyes. Then his hands were on her, gently pinching her nipples, his teeth nipping at her ear. She lay, her arms stretched across the edge of the tub as his hands played with her breasts and his mouth teased hers. Then his hands were between her legs. She opened her eyes and looked down but she couldn't see what he was doing through the bubbles.

It felt good. He touched and teased, yet she couldn't quite feel where his hands were at anytime. It was just a general sensation of being touched everywhere. She felt her nipples harden and her pussy swell. She wanted. Needed.

Then she was awake, staring into the darkened room,

feeling the warmth of Roger's body pressed against her side. She was lying with her arms stretched out at the shoulder and she could almost feel the edge of the hot tub. As the dream faded, she turned on her side and went back to sleep.

The following morning, she was up before the alarm and at Dr. Tannenbaum's office before eight. The first patient was early and was already in the operatory when Betsy arrived. The two women had little time to talk throughout the busy morning. At about eleven, Alice snagged Betsy as she passed. "Lunch?" she asked her friend. "We haven't had lunch together in a few weeks. How about it?"

"You sound like a woman with a purpose," Betsy said. "Have you come to a decision?"

"I think so but I need to talk to you."

"Okay. How about the diner?"

"Done."

By one-fifteen Betsy and Alice were seated in a booth and had ordered club sandwiches and Diet Cokes. "I did some reading last evening and that led to a lot of thinking. I'd like to give it a try but I'll need lots of help."

"Don't worry about that. I hope you won't mind but I already talked to Velvet and broached the idea about you taking a few calls. She'll need to meet you and chat, but I think it will work out. Her business is growing every month and she was already thinking about hiring another girl or two. You'd fit right in."

"How does it work, logistically, I mean?"

"Velvet has a pretty advanced computer system. Someone calls. If it's a prearranged appointment, the call goes directly to the right phone. If it's not, the person talks to the router and the caller can ask for the woman he wants to talk to. If she's available, then the call goes through. If she's not, then the caller can wait, in which case they pay while they are on hold. If he doesn't want to wait for a specific woman or if the caller is new to Velvet Whispers, there's a queuing system so it's the next available person. Some girls need a place to be, so they work at Velvet's house. Others, like me, work at our own homes but between the computer and the phone company, everyone gets paid."

"How many girls does Velvet have?"

"It varies. It's usually around a dozen."

"I never realized that there would be so many people doing this stuff."

"And Velvet's only one of thousands of phone services all around the country."

"Does she really charge three dollars a minute?"

"It seems like a lot, but many services charge more."

"I can't get over it. My cut would be almost a hundred bucks an hour." That number had been bouncing around in her brain since Betsy first told her about Velvet Whispers.

"I know. It still amazes me. I get to keep half, the router gets paid, and Velvet gets the rest."

"That seems fair. Is this legal?"

"Sure. It's not prostitution. Just a phone call."

The two women stopped talking as the waiter brought their sandwiches and drinks. When he turned toward another table Alice leaned forward and, sotto voce, asked, "What if a guy refuses to pay?" What if she tried it and was a flop?

"Velvet and the girl involved take the hit, of course, and he never gets to call again. Most men really enjoy the service and wouldn't jeopardize it by not paying the bill. Actually for some men who worry about the money, I have a timer that dings every fifteen minutes to keep them aware of the time. I don't want anyone to be surprised."

"Don't they want to call you directly? You know, cut out the middleman and pay you less."

"A few have suggested it, but I wouldn't dream of cutting Velvet out. Anyway, I don't want to give out my home number."

"Yeah, I understand. How many regular customers do you have?" Alice took a large bite of her sandwich.

"I take three hours of calls a night, that's usually between four and six callers. Some are prearranged, some just random. The first-time clients take a bit longer since I have to take my time and find out what they want." Betsy poured a lake of ketchup beside the french fries on her plate.

"That sounds really scary. What if they aren't satisfied?"

"There's no guarantee, of course, and they take that risk. Most men want pretty much the same things and they make their needs quite clear from the beginning."

"Lots of four letter words and adjectives?"

Betsy chuckled and chewed her fry. "Some. Others just want someone to talk to. Some want to tell *their* exploits, some want to talk about doing things their wives don't want to do, some just want to masturbate while you *watch*."

"Wives? Are they married? That never occurred to me. I thought most of them would he horny single guys with no one to play with."

"That's what I thought when I started. Lots of them, however, are men with wives they think wouldn't understand their desires. Some want to talk about bondage, spanking, or anal sex, things they think *nice girls* like their wives wouldn't be interested in."

"I see."

Betsy raised an inquiring eyebrow. "Want to meet Velvet?"

"I think I would."

"I'll set something up and let you know."

They continued to eat, and talked about other matters. Alice felt both light and terrified, and the feelings hadn't changed by the following Saturday afternoon when she pulled into the driveway of a small house in Putnam Valley. She had considered how to dress and had changed clothes after Dr. Tannenbaum's office closed. She had finally decided on a pair of tan slacks, a brown turtleneck sweater, and an oatmeal-colored wool jacket. As she walked up the driveway, she tried not to prejudge, but she knew that she had already created a mental image of Velvet that was surprisingly like the bosomy madam of old western movies. Over made up, slightly overdressed, with eyes that knew everything about men that there was to know.

The woman who answered the door couldn't have resembled her image less. "Hello. You must be Alice." She was dressed in jeans and a pale blue sweatshirt. "Obviously, I'm Velvet. Come on in." Alice followed in a daze. Velvet was in her mid-thirties, with carefully blow-dried hair and just a hint of makeup. She was about five foot six, and weighed only about a hundred and ten pounds. She was not particularly pretty, but she had large eyes that were so deep blue as to be almost black, with long lashes. And she was almost completely flat-chested. Why had Alice expected big breasts?

"I thought we could talk in the den," Velvet said, taking Alice's jacket and leading the way through a neat, tastefully furnished, split-level house. They walked through the living room to the back of the house and stopped at the doorway of a wood-paneled room furnished with two comfortable leather lounge chairs. The den was occupied by a boy of about Brandon's age, and a girl who looked to be about five. They were stretched out on the floor, the boy working on a half-built model car and the girl carefully coloring a picture of the Little Mermaid. "Matthew and Caitlin, say hello to Ms. Waterman."

"Hello, Ms. Waterman," the two said in unison.

"I need to use this room for a little while." She opened a closet above the TV and fished out a video. "How about *Milo and Otis*? You two can watch in my room while I talk with Ms. Waterman."

"That movie's dumb. Can I work on my car?"

"Put down lots of newspaper and be careful with the glue. Okay?"

"Okay." The boy gathered the pieces of his model and the rest of the paraphernalia and started toward the door.

"Can we have ice cream?" Caitlin asked.

"It's too close to dinnertime."

"Please. Pretty please with sugar on it." Alice could tell from Matthew's expression that he usually let Caitlin do the wheedling.

"No ice cream. Daddy's in the basement. Ask him to cut up an apple for each of you and you can take that and a can of soda upstairs. But don't spill."

"Thanks, Mommy," Caitlin said.

"And after the movie, can I play Nintendo?" Matthew added.

Velvet turned to Alice. "They both have great futures as negotiators." She turned back to her children. "Okay, if there's time. Now scoot."

The two bounced from the room, yelling, "Daddy, we get sodas."

Velvet grinned at the backs of her children. "They're a handful but I love them."

Alice's mind was boggled. She had just gotten used to her best friend, mother of her godchildren, being a phone-sex operator. Now this. Velvet wasn't at all what Alice had expected. "They are wonderful. I understand that Matthew is the same age as Brandon."

"They were born on the same day. Betsy and I treat ourselves to dinner the following week, just to prove we lived through the annual birthday parties the way we lived through childbirth." Alice and Velvet settled into the matched lounge chairs. "You look slightly like the deer caught in the headlights," Velvet said.

"I'm sorry. I've only known about you and everything for

about a week. It's still hard to wrap my mind around it all. You seem so . . ."

"Normal?"

"I guess. I'm sorry. I don't mean to be insulting."

"You're not, and I appreciate the honesty. Can I get you something to drink?"

"No, thanks."

"Why don't you tell me about yourself?"

For several minutes, Alice told Velvet about her life and about Ralph. She freely admitted that her marriage hadn't been a sexual revelation and that she was still somewhat naive. "I've been doing a lot of reading and my eyes are opening rather quickly."

"I'll bet. Betsy tells me you're something of a storyteller. She says you're very good at it."

"Yes. I guess so."

"I've been toying with an idea for several months and when Betsy called and told me about you, I thought you might just be the right person." Curious, Alice remained silent. "I've had several men ask me to tell them erotic stories. I've suggested that they read tales from books or from the Internet, but they said they wanted to hear really hot fantasies from the lips of a woman with a sexy voice."

"But you . . ."

"Not my thing. I'm good at different things." Velvet winked. "I can talk a man to orgasm really well." Velvet took a deep breath, dropped her shoulders and her chin and said, "Sometimes I have just the sexy voice they are looking for." Her voice had changed completely. It was soft, breathy, and lower pitched. Alice knew that if she were a man, that voice would go right through her.

"How do you do that?"

"It's really not difficult. I'll show you. Do you think you could make up really hot stories? You could write them beforehand, but your client might ask for something special.

You'd have to be able to think on your feet."

"I don't know. I hadn't thought about it."

"It would make things a bit easier for you until you get the hang of this."

"I guess it would be easier." Alice had thought about having to personally interact with the men on the phone, verbally being part of the sex, and that had felt like the most difficult part. Now Velvet had thought of another way. Prewritten stories.

"It would mean that you wouldn't get too many men 'off the street.' Most would be prearranged because of your specialty and it might lower your financial expectations. I gather you need the money to help your mom."

"I need about four hundred a month to get her into the best nursing home in Westchester."

Alice could see Velvet quickly calculate. "That shouldn't be a problem. Here's what I would suggest. How about writing a few stories and letting me read them? That will give me an idea of how well you express the things that men want to hear."

"That sounds like a good way to begin," Alice said, "and it takes some of the pressure off me." That way she wouldn't have to get on the phone until she was sure she could please the client. The thought of failure terrified her.

"Then we can see where we'll go from there. How about coming over next Saturday afternoon, same time and I'll read what you've written? Or, if you write something sooner you could mail it to me. I don't want to rush you, but I gather you're under some time pressure."

Alice and her sister had found an upcoming spot in a second-tier nursing home, but were still waiting to hear from Rutlandt. The current arrangement would work for another three weeks, then they would have to make a decision. "I guess Betsy told you the whole story."

"She did, and I'm really sorry. Both of my parents and

both of Wayne's are still alive and, as they age, their future concerns me."

"I'll write what I can this week, and then be back same time next Saturday and we can talk more."

"Wonderful. Betsy's one of my favorite people and I'm glad to help."

"Don't do it just for her."

"I wouldn't dream of it. This is my business and the source of all our savings. I wouldn't jeopardize it for anyone. If I don't think you'll work out, I'll tell you."

"Thanks. I just need for you to be honest."

The two women stood and Velvet handed Alice her jacket. They walked to the front door and, as she stepped into the clear late-afternoon sunshine, Velvet quickly kissed her on the cheek. "Write up a storm."

"I will, and thanks for the chance."

Chapter 5

As she drove home, Alice thought about everything Velvet had said, and realized that, as naive as she might be in her personal life, she was creative enough to give this a real try. It wasn't going to be easy, but they didn't pay big bucks because what she was trying to do was easy. It was late in the afternoon and the sun was low in the sky. Although it was late March, there was no real hint of spring yet, so as she drove, Alice turned the heater up a notch.

Heat. That was what she needed to create in any story she wrote. She'd always been good in English composition and had gotten lots of *A*'s on her writing in high school, but this wasn't high school. Not by a long shot. Oh well. She had nothing to lose.

When she arrived home, she turned on her computer and browsed the Net. She was becoming familiar with a few of the picture sites and she gazed with a clinical eye at the photos. Most of them didn't excite her, but she found that a few, involving people being tied up, made her uneasy in a not unpleasant way. She tried to think like a researcher and assumed that most of the sites were aimed at males. She gleaned lots of pointers from what the webmasters thought would appeal to men and read lots of text that was supposed to be arousing.

How could she be sure what would turn a guy on? She hadn't a clue but, she reasoned, if it made her feel sexy, then it just might work. After several hours on the Net, she finally logged off.

What to write about? *Can I do a story about straight sex? Would anyone be interested in just a man and a woman making love? There has to be lots of hands and oral sex at least,* she thought. *Lots of sucking and stroking. Can I write about oral sex even though I've never done it?* Well, she reasoned, many people write about things they've never done.

She booted up the word processor she used for occasional letters and stared at the blank screen. She typed a few sentences, then deleted them. She got as far as the first paragraph, then stared, shook her head, and again blanked her screen. After half an hour of fruitless staring, she called Betsy and filled her in on her visit with Velvet. "She's such a nice person it's hard to believe she does what she does," Alice said.

"I know. It's sometimes hard for me to believe I do what I do."

"I didn't mean to sound insulting."

"You didn't. Are you going to write tonight?"

She turned so her back was to the computer. "I'm going to try. I've been trying."

"I know you can do it, so I won't hold you up. Get cracking. See you Monday morning."

Alice hung up and her eyes returned to the blank word-processing screen in front of her. She thought for several minutes, then got up, went into the kitchen, and made herself a bite of dinner. With a cup of soup, an American-cheese sandwich and a Coke on a tray, she returned to the desk in her bedroom. She ate and stared at the screen. When she was finished eating, she took the tray back into the kitchen and washed her plate and cup and the dirty dishes left over from the day before. Then she sponged off every surface and scoured the sink.

Roger jumped onto the counter and chirruped at her. "Okay. I know, Roger," she said, carrying the cat back into the bedroom. "I'm stalling." When he again chirruped, she continued, "Don't yell at me. I just don't know whether I can do this. It's so embarrassing." Why was it embarrassing? She was alone in the apartment. No one would read anything she wrote unless she chose to show it to them. Whatever she created was hers. Private.

Alice began to write, using several stories from the Internet as models and adding her own reactions and feelings. She wrote for more than two hours, reread, and edited what she had written, then turned to Roger, now curled in a ball on the bed. "This is really weird. It embarrasses me just to read what I wrote but I think it's not too bad. Not great, but maybe not too bad." She ran her spell-checking program, then printed out the six pages. The next step was to find out whether she could actually say the words out loud. She sat on the bed beside the cat. "Okay. Here goes."

THE BEIGE TRENCH COAT

Jenny loved to read and whenever she had a moment to pick up a book, she did. One evening she had a few minutes while her husband and her three children tried to fix their broken dishwasher, so she sat in the lounge chair in the living room and read several pages of a novel. The part she read involved the heroine showing up at a guy's office wearing only her mink coat. There followed a delightfully graphic description of the interlude during which the heroine and her latest conquest made love on the desk, his secretary just a few feet and one closed door away.

"Man, oh man," Jenny whispered as she read the scene for a second time. "I wish I could be like that, aggressive and sexy."

"Hey, Mom," her daughter yelled, "I think we found the problem. Remember those toothpick critters we made? Well, it looks like Robbie dumped a few in the dishwasher. They jammed this hoodingy here. Come check this out." Reluctantly, Jenny put her book down and "checked out" the dishwasher.

A few hours later Jenny was in bed, watching the eleven o'clock news when her husband, Len, came upstairs. "Hon," he said, "you left this in the living room." He entered the bedroom holding the novel open to the page Jenny had been reading. "This is really hot stuff."

"Damn. I forgot it. I'm glad you found it not one of the kids."

"Me too. This is really explicit."

"That is quite a scene, isn't it."

"Sure is. That's some lucky guy."

"He is?"

"Sure. Sexy broad comes to his office hot to trot. What do you think?"

Jenny arched her back and looked down at her moderate-size bosom, filling out the top of her lacy nightgown. "It would have to be someone really sexy for a guy to take chances like that. I mean with his secretary right there in the next room."

"Nah. Just the idea of something like that," he paused and looked down at the bulge in the front of his sweatpants, "you know, dangerous, would make any guy hot." Len came around to Jenny's side of the bed, pulled off his clothes, and made quick, hungry love to his wife.

Later, as she lay listening to her husband's breathing return to normal, Jenny thought again about the scene that had made Len so excited. *I wonder,* she thought.

By the end of the following week, Jenny had made all her plans. She had taken the afternoon off and selected her wardrobe. Around 3:00 P.M., she arrived at her husband's office, dressed in a beige trench coat. "Paula," she said to Len's secretary who was busily typing into a word processor, "I've got to talk to Len about something in private. Will you hold all his calls until we let you know otherwise? And don't let anyone interrupt."

"Sure thing, Jenny," Paula said. "Nothing wrong, I hope."

"Nothing at all, Paula," Jenny said. "We just need a little time for some private business."

"Will do," Paula said.

Jenny entered Len's small private office, quietly closed the door behind her and turned the lock. Len was fiddling with some files in his credenza so his back was to her. For a moment, Jenny almost changed her mind. Would he really find this exciting? Would she make a fool of herself? She rubbed her sweaty palms on her coat and crossed to the desk.

"Hi, Len," she said, making her voice low and throaty.

"Hi, hon," Len said, turning in his swivel chair, a folder in his hand. "What are you doing here?"

"Well, I, ah . . ."

"I am glad to see you but I'm really busy. And why aren't you at work? Is something wrong?"

"No, nothing's wrong. It's just . . ." Again Jenny ran her shaking hands down her coat.

"Honey, what's wrong?"

Slowly, before what little courage she had deserted her completely, she unbuttoned her coat and pulled the sides open. Beneath she wore only a black satin bra and panties, a garter belt, black stockings with lace tops and black high-heeled shoes. Silent, she stared at her husband. She watched surprise and shock flash across his face, then a slow smile spread over his mouth.

He cleared his throat. "It's that scene from that book," he said hoarsely.

"Yes," she said softly, "it is."

"Oh," he said, he breathing increasing. "Wow."

Encouraged by the look on her husband's face, Jenny slowly let the trench coat slide from her arms. "I hope you like what you see," she said, echoing the heroine's line from the book.

"Oh, baby, I certainly do. Come over here."

Mimicking the scene from the book seemed to make it easier for Jenny to climb out of herself. "Not so fast, baby," she said hoarsely. "This is my party." She pranced around the office, wiggling her hips and humming "The Stripper." "Do you like?"

Len sat and stared. "I like this very much, but I'm really waiting for a very important phone call so get over here right now." He made a grab for her but she neatly avoided his grasp. "Come on, baby," he almost whined.

"In due time."

The intercom on the phone beeped. "Baby . . ."

This part hadn't been in the scene from the book so Jenny sighed and said, "Maybe you'd better get that."

"Yes," Len said as he put the receiver to his ear.

Jenny settled herself on Len's lap and could hear Paula's voice clearly. "I'm sorry, Len, but Mr. Haverstraw is on the line and he's leaving his office soon. I know that your wife didn't want you two to be disturbed, but I thought you would want to take this call."

Jenny could hear Len's deep sigh. "I guess I have to," he said, wiggling out from under Jenny's almost-bare behind. He covered the mouthpiece with his hand. "Baby, just hold that sexy thought for about five minutes. Okay?"

"Sure," Jenny said, deflated.

Len pushed the lighted button on his phone. "Mr. Haverstraw. I'm glad to finally get to talk to you."

Jenny sat in a chair on the opposite side of Len's desk and pondered. What would the woman in the book have done? Certainly not just sit here. An idea formed in Jenny's head and for several minutes she argued with herself, then decided. *The hell with it. I'm going to go for it.*

Now paying no attention to his wife, Len was furiously making notes on a yellow pad.

Slowly, Jenny made her way around the desk and, as Len distractedly made room for her, she wiggled under the desk. With trembling hands, she quickly unzipped Len's pants and pulled out his flaccid cock. She cradled it in her hand and watched it come to life.

Len pushed his chair back and stared at Jenny sitting in the kneehole. With his hand against the mouthpiece, he whispered, "Baby, please . . ." He pushed the chair back against the desk and Jenny could hear his pen scratching on the pad. She leaned forward and took Len's now semierect cock between her lips and sucked it into her warm mouth.

She heard Len gasp, then hiss, "Stop that!" Then he said, "No Mr. Haverstraw, not you. No, there's nothing wrong."

Smiling, Jenny sucked. This was extra delicious, she realized. Since Len had to continue his conversation, she would continue her ministrations as well. She fondled and sucked, then reached into his pants and squeezed his testicles.

"Mr. Haverstraw," Len said, his voice hoarse and tentative. "We're having some, er, electrical problems here. Can I call you back?" There was a pause. "Yes, I think I have enough to begin a rough estimate."

Jenny flicked her tongue over the tip of Len's cock, then pulled the thick, hard member into her mouth again.

"Yes, I'll get back to you tomorrow."

When she heard Len hang up, she slid from under the

desk. Len grabbed her and spun her around, pushing her down so she was bent over his desk, papers and pens flying in all directions. With one quick movement, he ripped off her panties and plunged his hard cock into her steaming pussy. "God, I'm so hot," she moaned.

"Me too," Len said, grasping Jenny's hips and forcing her even more tightly against his groin. "God, baby."

It took only a few thrusts for Len to shoot his load into his wife's hot cunt, making strangling sounds, trying not to yell. Then he reached around and rubbed Jenny's clit until she came, almost silently.

"Len," Paula said through the locked door, "is everything all right?"

Len cleared his throat, Jenny still bent over the desk. "Everything's just great, Paula."

Len collapsed into his desk chair and pulled his wife onto his lap, then kissed her deeply. "I can't believe you did that," he said finally.

Jenny giggled. "I can't either." She got up from Len's lap and grabbed a wad of tissues from her purse. "Was I too outrageous?"

"Oh, baby. It was difficult there for a while, and I'll have to make a few excuses to Haverstraw, but it was wonderful."

Jenny picked up the coat and put it back on. "Yeah, it was, wasn't it." After a few more kisses, she unlocked the door and walked out. "We're done, for the moment, Paula."

"That's great, Jenny," Paula said. "I hope everything worked out."

"Oh yes," Jenny and Len said, almost simultaneously, "it certainly did work out."

"God. I actually got through it," Alice said, stacking the pages of her story. "What do you think, Roger? Does that make it?" She looked at the cat, who was now fast asleep, and giggled. "I hope you're not a good judge of quality."

Initially she had strangled on the more graphic words, but she had eventually said them all, and the more often she said them, the easier they became. "I can say *clit* and *pussy* and *cock*. I've come a long way, baby." She giggled again, then laughed out loud. "If Ralph could only see me now."

The following day was Sunday, so after a quick visit to Queens, Alice spent the rest of the day either writing or surfing the Internet for ideas. She worked until almost midnight and, by the time she climbed into bed, she had written three more stories. The following morning she put them all in a large brown envelope and dropped them off at the post office on her way to work.

The week dragged. Alice visited her mother and sister on Wednesday and on the drive to Queens, she worked out exactly what she was going to tell her family. "I think I might have a really exciting new job one or two nights a week," she told her sister and brother-in-law.

"Doing what?" Sue asked.

"Phone sales," Alice answered, as she had rehearsed. "It's a bit complicated to explain, but it pays really well and I don't have to sell anything I don't believe in." She almost choked on the last phrase, but she hoped she would cover all the bases so there wouldn't be any awkward questions. "Any luck with Rutlandt?" she asked, changing the subject as quickly as she could.

"I got a letter from them. They have Mom at the top of the waiting list but they have no way of knowing when they will have an opening. I don't know whether we can afford it." Sue looked like she was coping as best she could, but it was difficult for both of them.

Alice patted her sister's hand. "I'll have a better idea by Saturday, when I find out about this new job. If it pans out, we'll be okay." If Velvet gave her the go-ahead, she'd empty her meager savings if she had to and replace the money as she got paid.

"Then I'll keep my fingers crossed for you."

Alice held up her hands, all fingers linked to others. "I've got everything crossed but my eyes."

She tried not to count on the job too much but the following Saturday afternoon she had her heart in her mouth as she drove to Velvet's house. As she had the previous week, Velvet, dressed as Alice was, in jeans and a man-tailored shirt, escorted her into the den, this week free of children. "They're at the movies with Wayne. You didn't meet Wayne the last time you were here, did you?"

"No." Alice was having difficulty focusing on Velvet's conversation.

Velvet picked up Alice's envelope and paced as she talked. "I'm sorry. Let's get to it. The stories are sensational."

Alice let out a long sigh of relief. "Do you really think so?"

"I do. You've got just the right amount of hot sex without the raunchy stuff that Velvet Whispers usually avoids. There are so many 'You phone, I'll pretend to suck you off' phone services that we try for something a bit more upscale and our clients have responded. I have a few guys who will love this stuff."

"That's wonderful."

"I know this must come as a relief to you. I've been giving this a lot of thought and I have one idea. It would sound more personal if the stories from a woman's point of view were in first person. Like 'I did this and that.' They could sound like they were personal revelations that you've never told anyone before. The ones from a man's might be stories someone told you. Personal tales, not something someone made up. I think that would go over better. What do you think?"

Alice considered Velvet's suggestion for only a moment. "You're right, of course. I'm annoyed that I didn't think of that."

"Great. Now here's my idea. We'll call you Sheherazade

and I'll tell a few guys that you're a new erotic storyteller I've found. They might want to hear something specific, like," Velvet tapped her front teeth as she thought, "like the first time you made love or something naughty you did last week. You could write them out in advance but you'd have to roll with it from time to time. You'll have to be able to think fast and vary the story to go along with their ideas and desires." Alice could see the wheels turning as Velvet created her identity. Sheherazade's Secrets.

The more Velvet talked, the more it seemed to Alice that she might be able to make it all work. "Can you say this stuff out loud?" Velvet asked.

Alice smiled. "Well, I've read all these stories to my cat, if that counts. After listening to these tales I'll bet he's the hottest animal in town."

"Great," Velvet said with a chuckle. "This might just make us each some money. Let me make a few calls to men who I think would be interested, and I'll see what I can set up. Are you willing to get started next week?"

Next week! "I'm game." She took a deep breath. "Let's do it."

"Wonderful. I'll call you midweek and we'll nail down the specifics. What nights do you want to work, for now?"

"I thought about Mondays, Wednesdays, and Fridays. Are the weekends your busiest times? I could work Saturdays too."

"You know, it varies. Some weekends it seems the entire male population of the world calls, and others it's really silent. You get fifty percent of whatever the callers are charged, based only on actual time on the phone, of course. The usual rate is $2.99 per minute. I'd like you to get a timer that will ding every ten minutes so those who care will know how much they're paying. For the most part, however, I've found that most of these guys don't give a damn."

"How long should the calls go? I know Betsy said some of hers go more than half an hour."

"Yours will too," Velvet said. "It should take twenty minutes to half an hour to read a seven- or eight-page story, more if your tales get longer or if you talk slowly. If someone wants to limit the amount of money he spends, you can suggest that you can continue the story next week. You'll have to take notes and pick up just where you left off. Your clients will remember every detail." Velvet continued to think out loud. "To create regular customers, you might want to have some of your stories continued, like X-rated soap operas. Everyone should get off in each segment, but you can reuse the same characters. That's all up to you."

"Do you want me to start with someone who's not a paying customer to make sure that you like what I'm doing?"

"We can if you like," Velvet said, her smile warm and open, "but I'm confident that you can do this."

Suddenly unsure, Alice asked, "How can you be so sure? You don't know me at all."

"Actually, I do. I know you through these wonderful stories you wrote, and I've talked about you with Betsy several times this week. We both think it will work out wonderfully well for you. Anything else?"

"I'd like to start with only one or two people and test it all out. I don't want you to make any promises we can't keep."

"That sounds fine with me." She stood up and walked Alice to the front door. As Alice stepped out onto the porch, Velvet said, "Go get 'em, Sherry."

"Sheherazade. Sherry. I like that." With a quick motion, she kissed Velvet on the cheek. "Thanks."

"You're certainly welcome. And I'm not a charity. We're both going to make some nice bucks out of this. I'll call you."

Alice called Betsy as soon as she got home and filled

her in on the meeting with Velvet. "She's a love."

"She certainly is, and, with the women she's got working for her and very little overhead, she makes a really nice living too."

"I'll bet. I've got stories to write now. I want a few of every type that men might ask for. Give me some clues. What kind of sex do men want from their encounters?"

"Most of my clients enjoy the idea of a woman performing oral sex on them. I guess it's something that their wives won't do."

"Oh. Don't women like that sort of thing?"

"I guess not. Did you and Ralph . . ."

"No. He was just a missionary position kind of guy. Do you and Larry?"

"Of course. It's wonderful. You might think about having sex in semipublic places, too, for your stories. I have a few clients who love the idea of possibly being found out. And of course, you need lots of control stories."

"I know. I've read a lot of those, where the men almost rape the women."

"Don't overlook the men who want to be dominated too. Oh, and one more thing: Men love to think about two women making love. Lesbian sex seems to turn guys on."

Alice was taken aback. She had never considered that men might want such a thing. "Phew. I don't know about that."

"You don't have to *do* it, just talk about it. I do. Several times I've told stories about my supposed adventures with another woman."

Alice gasped. "Have you ever?"

"No. But I can invent stories and before you say it, no, it's not lying. These men know who and what you are. It's the fantasy they're after, not the reality of who you really are. They understand. It's just a way for them to get off."

After Alice hung up, she booted up her computer and began to type. For the rest of the weekend, except for her visit to her sister's, she did nothing but write, edit, and rewrite. When she temporarily ran out of ideas, she prowled the Internet, not stealing stories, just getting her mind loosened up.

On Monday evening, she got a call from Velvet. "I talked to a man named Vic. He's a really sweet guy who's always asking me to tell him about my lurid past. I told him about Sheherazade and he's really psyched. He'd like to call you on Wednesday evening at about nine. Would that work for you?"

Vic. Her first client. Alice's hands trembled and she could barely get out the words, "That would be fine."

"I know you're probably nervous, but try not to be. He's just a really nice, sort of shy guy who just enjoys getting his rocks off once a week with a dirty conversation. And he's got the money to be able to do just that."

Alice barked out a rueful laugh. "He's shy and I'm terrified. What a pair we'll make."

"You'll do fine. He usually stays on the phone for about half an hour. That's forty-five dollars for you for just a short bit of work. Think of it that way if it makes it easier."

"Is there anything special he wants in my story?"

"He likes hot, aggressive women who like a bit of danger. That's about all I can think of."

Alice thought about a story she'd just finished. "Actually that will work out nicely."

"Good. I told him to call me right after he talks to you so he can let me know how he likes you and whether he wants to call again next week. Then I'll call you. If you both think it went well, he'll become as regular as he wants. We can use him as a sort of test case. If it works out, I'll see who else I can set you up with."

"Great. It's kind of like the ultimate job interview."

Velvet's laugh was warm and comforting. "I know you'll be great. A few tips. When you talk, deliberately relax your shoulders and drop both the pitch and volume of your voice. Get just a bit of breath into it, but don't get all Mae West or Marilyn Monroe either. You might want to have a few beers before he calls, just to relax you."

After a few more minutes, the two women hung up and Alice reread the story she thought Vic might like. *This might just please him,* she thought.

All week Alice was in a tizzy. She talked with Betsy almost incessantly, looking for reassurance. The women met Wednesday for lunch and Alice asked Betsy several times whether she thought that her storytelling would work. Over coffee Betsy finally said, "I think I'm going to strangle you. If you don't want to do this, then don't. If you do, then just take your chances and do it. If it all falls apart and you're terrible, you're no worse off than you would have been if it had never happened."

"I guess that's right." Alice smiled and winked at her friend. "Thanks. I needed that."

On her way home from lunch, Alice bought a six-pack of Budweiser. She didn't particularly like beer and she hated the calories that went with it, but tonight she'd need to unwind. The afternoon dragged by and she was sorry that her first call had been planned for a Wednesday, the only day during the week that she didn't work. At least at Dr. Tannenbaum's office the day would pass more quickly. As it was, the afternoon seemed about three days long.

Alice sipped a beer with dinner, one for dessert, and yet another at about eight-thirty. Like medicine, she told herself. When the phone rang at nine o'clock, she was seated on the edge of the bed, just slightly buzzed. She listened to the first ring, then picked it up on the second. "Hello?"

"Is this Sheherazade?"

"Yes," she said, her heart pounding. "You must be Vic."

"That's me. How are you tonight?"

"I'm fine. I've been waiting for your call. I have a story for you that you might enjoy."

"That's great. First, tell me what you look like."

"Tonight, I'm twenty-five, slim, with 36D breasts and long legs."

She heard a deep breath. "That's great," Vic said. "Blond hair and blue eyes?"

"Why yes," Alice said, putting a bit of surprise in her voice. "How did you know?"

"I guess I'm just lucky. That's the way I like to picture women."

Alice made a few notes on the pad beside her. "That's really lucky. I'm glad I'm just what you wanted."

"Are you ready to tell me your story, Sheherazade?"

"Oh yes. I love telling stories about all the women inside of me."

"Okay. I'm putting my feet up and I'm ready."

Alice picked up the pages she had written. She'd use them as a guideline, and improvise when she had to.

Chapter 6

"You know, Vic, I have a secret. I love tollbooths. I know that's a ridiculous statement, but after you've heard my story, I think you'll understand. It happened a while ago, but I still remember it.

"Let me back up. Throughout college, I loved to wear tight jeans, and sweaters cut just low enough to reveal my cleavage. I enjoyed the way guys in my classes looked at me. I developed a clumsy way of dropping my books so I could bend over and watch them as they watched me.

"When I graduated, I got a job as a secretary in a large, very formal accounting firm. It was all terribly gray-flannel: women in tailored suits worn with blouses buttoned up to the neck. Each morning, I put my long hair up, using dozens of pins to keep it neat. By the end of each day, all I could think about was taking my clothes off, unpinning my hair, and relaxing. But the work was interesting and the pay was great so I put up with the minor disadvantages. You know how it can be."

"Oh yes," Vic said. "I do. I used to work in a place like that myself."

"Then you do understand. Well, after almost a year, I treated myself to a tiny red convertible. Instead of taking the commuter train, I started to drive to work every morning on the parkway, my blouse primly buttoned and my hair up. Unhappily, I had to keep the top of the car closed or the wind would have ruined my appearance.

"On the way home, however, I was under no such restrictions. I could unbutton, unpin, and unwind. After a few weeks, the weather turned warm and I decided to lower the top of my car for the drive home. The spring air was soft and warm one afternoon so I removed my jacket and unbuttoned my blouse. Then I took five minutes and pulled every pin out of my hair, until it fell in soft waves down my back. I felt free."

"Was it long and blond?"

"Of course. A soft yellow like . . ." she struggled for a phrase, "new wheat."

"Wow."

"So that afternoon I shifted into first and eased my car out of the garage and into traffic. As I drove along the parkway toward my apartment I was exhilarated by the feel of the wind in my hair and down the front of my blouse. I could feel my nipples harden under the silky fabric. I pulled into the line of traffic and, quarter in hand, I slowly inched my way toward the tollbooth just before my exit. As I reached out to put the quarter in the outstretched hand, I glanced at the toll taker. What do you look like, Vic?"

"I'm about thirty-five, with brown hair and brown eyes."

"Do you have a nice body?"

"It's not much," Vic said softly.

"Oh, I'll bet it is. I'll bet you have nice shoulders, just like the toll taker. I remember him. He had great shoulders. Do you have good hands?"

"I never thought about it. I guess I do."

"Wonderful. Just like him. So each evening, I drove home the same way. About a week later, I found myself gazing at the same guy. Brown hair, brown eyes, and great shoulders and hands." She sighed. "Anyway, as he took my quarter, he looked me over and then he squeezed my hand. I smiled at him and pulled away.

"For the next few days, I made sure to be in his lane. Each day, I gave him a better view of my body. I began to deliberately hike up my skirt and pull my blouse open so he could see my low-cut bra."

"You did?"

"Oh yes. I loved it that he liked looking at me. By the end of the third week, I realized that I was wet just thinking about my drive home. I said hello to him each night and he stared down my blouse and said hello too.

"One evening I casually asked him when his shift was over. 'Midnight,' he told me. That was just what I wanted to hear.

"Well, Vic. You'll never guess what I did. The following evening, I had dinner near my office and returned to work. I had a desk full of things that needed my attention so I had no trouble finding enough work to keep me busy until almost eleven. When I could concentrate no longer, I stretched, rubbed the back of my neck, and smiled. I was going to be so bad.

"When I got to my car, the garage was almost empty and the corner I had parked in was not well lit. I glanced around and saw no one so I quickly pulled off my skirt and my half-slip. I glanced down at my sheer black stockings and black garter belt topped by tiny black bikini panties. Can you picture it, Vic?"

"Oh yes. I'll bet you looked sexy."

"I think I did. As I slid into the car I enjoyed the feel of the leather upholstery on the backs of my thighs and the slithery feeling of my soaking cunt. I had put a large silk scarf in the car that morning and now I pulled it across my lap, covering me up to the bottom of my blouse. My show was for only one man.

"It was almost 11:45 when I lowered the top of the car and drove through the warm spring air toward the toll plaza. As I drove up to the booth I could see the familiar face as he stretched to take money from a car in front of me. I unbuttoned my blouse all the way and pulled it open to reveal my black lace half-bra that barely covered my nipples. I moved the scarf over onto the passenger seat and pulled up next to him.

"Distractedly he leaned out to take my toll, but when he saw me, he just stared. It was the most beautiful look I've ever received. His eyes caressed every inch of my skin until I couldn't sit still any longer. Fortunately there were no other cars around so, as he watched, I slipped my hand between my legs and stroked my wet pussy through the thin crotch of my tiny panties. It took only a moment until I came, waves of orgasm engulfing my body. When I calmed and looked at him, I could tell that he wanted to touch me, but his fingers couldn't quite reach."

"Oh, wow. That's fantastic," Vic said.

"That's what he thought too. 'I get off at midnight,' he said. 'Why not save some of that for me?'

"'Where?' I asked.

"Quickly he wrote an address on a piece of paper and handed it to me. I'll wait for you in front of my building at about twelve-fifteen.' "

"Did you go?" Vic asked, his voice hoarse.

"I hadn't decided yet, I guess. Without saying yes or no, I drove away, my quarter and his address in my hand. As soon as I got to an exit, I turned off of the parkway, pulled my car to a stop, and considered. I was still high and hungry. I rubbed my soaked crotch until I came again, but the orgasm was unsatisfying. I needed a cock inside of me, preferably his. I guess I had made the decision before I even left work that night.

"So I buttoned my blouse, wriggled into my skirt as best I could and drove to the address the man had written down. I didn't even know his name, Vic, but I guess I didn't care."

"You actually did it? Met him?"

"I did. He drove up at exactly twelve-fifteen and I got out of my car. 'I don't even know your name,' we said simultaneously.

"I didn't want to tell him my real name so I made one up. 'Mine's Christine,' I said.

"You know," Alice said to Vic. " I just remembered. His name was Vic too."

"Really?" Vic said.

"Oh yes. 'I'm Vic,' he said. 'Come on. I'll let us in.' "

"I know his name wasn't Vic, but I like it this way," the phone voice said. "Go on."

"The apartment was small and inexpensively furnished but I barely got a chance to look around. We got inside and, without waiting, Vic wrapped his arms around me and his lips engulfed my mouth. He tangled his hands in my hair and held my head while his tongue invaded and explored. He pressed his body against mine and I could feel his huge dick pressing against my belly. I wrapped my arms around his neck and surrendered to his kiss.

"His hands roamed my back, pressing my full breasts harder against his chest. It was as though he wanted to pull me inside of his skin.

"I slowly pulled away and looked into Vic's eyes. 'You enjoyed watching me before so let's not change things just yet,' I said."

Alice switched the phone to her other ear. "Vic. Would you like to hear about how I stripped in the story?"

"Oh yes. Very much," he said.

"Well. I unbuttoned his shirt and pressed my toll taker into an easy chair. I ran my hands over his chest, loosened his belt, and unsnapped his jeans. Then I backed away.

"One button at a time, I unfastened my black silk blouse. I watched his eyes. They never left my fingers as I played with my buttons.

"He reached out and tried to rush me but I pushed his hands away. 'This is my show,' I told him. 'Just be patient.'"

It was obvious to Alice that Vic was getting into the tale. "Can you be patient, Vic?"

"I'll be patient," he said into the phone.

"I'm sure you will. My toll taker sat, looked into my eyes and smiled. 'Just don't take too long,' he said. 'I may be able to wait, but I'm not sure about my cock.' "

Alice could hear Vic's warm laugh. "I opened the side button on my skirt and let it fall to the ground. I hadn't put my slip back on, so I could watch him stare at my nylon-encased legs and tiny panties. I slipped my blouse off, dropped it next to my skirt, and watched his eyes as they roamed my body.

"I began to run my hands over my belly and breasts. I stroked my nipples through the satin and lace of my bra. I ran my fingers over the soaked crotch of my panties. I closed my eyes and let my fingertips drift over my skin.

"After a few moments, I pulled my long hair forward, over my shoulders and breasts, then I unhooked my bra and pulled it off. The strands of hair parted only slightly, just enough to allow my erect nipples to protrude."

Alice heard a long-drawn-out sigh and a whispered, "Yes."

"I swayed slightly, enjoying the feel of my hair as it brushed back and forth across my breasts. Suddenly, showing Vic my body wasn't enough. I needed his hands and mouth on me.

"I knelt down in front of Vic's chair, looked up at him and smiled. He reached down, pulled my hair out of the way and took my breasts in his hands.

"His fingers found my hard nipples and he squeezed, tiny pinches that sent shivers up my spine. He pulled me up so my tits were level with his mouth and he licked the hard buds with the tip of his tongue. He swirled his tongue around and flicked it back and forth, wetting and teasing me. He leaned back slightly and blew on my wet skin. The sensation almost made me climax, but I held it back. This wasn't how I wanted to come.

"When I just couldn't wait any longer," Alice said, "I pulled him to his feet and almost ripped off his jeans. He was magnificent naked, with his hard cock beckoning me. I needed him inside me.

"'Take off those panties,' Vic said, 'but leave the rest on. I like you that way.'

"I pulled my panties off as he sat back down in the chair and grabbed my arms. I half dropped, half fell onto his lap, facing him. He lifted me slightly and then drove my body down, impaled on his huge cock."

Alice could hear the rasping sound of Vic's breathing through the phone. She trembled, feeling like the woman in the story. Brazen and able to ask for what she wanted. Able to do anything. "'Yes, fuck me,' I screamed as he penetrated me. 'Fuck me hard.'

"He wrapped his hands around my waist and rhythmically lifted and dropped me. My knees were buried in the deep chair cushions, my hands held his hair. He pounded inside of me until we both came, screaming."

Suddenly there was a loud gasp through the phone, then an, "Oh, shit."

"Is anything wrong, Vic?" Alice said.

"No. Not really. I just don't like to come so fast."

There was a long pause during which Alice couldn't stop grinning. She had done it. She had made a man come just from her words. *I really am hot stuff.*

"Did you ever see him again?"

"We met at his place occasionally for a night of hot sex but eventually he moved to the west coast."

"That was wonderful. Sheherazade, can I call you again next week? Please. Can you tell me more about your history?" He paused. "I know they're just stories, but I want to hear more."

"Of course. I'd love to tell you lots of tales about my past. Is there any kind of story you'd particularly like to hear?"

"Oh, no. I'll let you pick. And thanks."

"I'm glad you called and I'll look forward to hearing from you next week, at the same time."

She heard Vic hang up, and Alice dropped on the bed, pounded her fists, and kicked her heels. "Yes!" she yelled. "Yes!"

A half an hour later, the phone rang again. "Vic was delighted," Velvet said without preamble. "He said you were just the right kind of a slut for him." When Alice gasped, Velvet continued, "He meant it as a compliment. He loved hearing about your supposed lurid past." She chuckled. "I gather you took my advice and moved into first person."

"Did he really believe I had done what I told him in the story?"

"Probably not, but who knows, and who cares. He loved what you said and wants to call you again next week, and that's the only testimonial I care about. I've got a few more men I can recommend. How about Monday evening? I think I can set up two or three, starting at about eight. Would that work?"

"Would it? That would be terrific."

Velvet took a few minutes to tell Alice about the men she had in mind. "I'll call you over the weekend and make it official. Welcome to the family."

"Thanks."

After she hung up with Velvet, Alice called Sue. After a few pleasantries and the news that her mother was essentially unchanged, Alice said, "If Rutlandt calls, tell them yes."

"You got the job?" Sue shrieked. "That's great. I hope you aren't taking on too much."

"Not at all," Alice said, hating to deceive her sister. "I'm really going to enjoy what I'll be doing."

"That's fantastic. I'll call Rutlandt tomorrow and tell them that we're a go whenever they have a room. They said last Friday that they thought there'd be something this week."

The following Monday evening, a man named Scott called for a story. Velvet had told Alice that he would probably like a story about a man being educated by older women. Alice had decided that he'd want it told from the boy's point of view so over the weekend she had given a lot of thought to how to pull it off. Finally, Sunday evening she had had an idea, so after she and Scott had chatted for a few minutes, Alice said, "You know, Velvet said you might like to hear about my brother. He had an experience, well, he was very naughty. He told me in confidence but I don't think he'd mind if I told you."

"Really? Tell me."

"I have to tell you that Carter, that's my brother, wasn't very knowledgeable at all. My family was extremely protective and he had been more sheltered than most boys. He was also rather unattractive and painfully shy. He was just eighteen years old and a senior in high school when his first time happened, and it happened on a snowy winter weekend. He used to shovel driveways to earn extra money.

"He had already done two that afternoon so he was really exhausted. His last driveway was owned by a female customer who was unmarried and quite well to do. Let's call her Mrs. Jones. This particular afternoon, she invited him in and asked him to sit down and have something to eat. 'Lord knows your parents don't seem to feed you, so someone should,' she said.

"He was wet and shivering as he sat down at the table in her kitchen. 'They feed me, but I'm always hungry,' he said.

"'Carter, your clothes are wet and you're chilled straight through. Why don't you take off those wet things? I'll put them in the dryer and you can wrap yourself in this big towel.' She handed him a tremendous bath towel and hustled him into the bathroom.'"

Alice dropped her voice to a slight whisper. "We know he shouldn't have taken off all his clothes, but he was so naive."

"Maybe he wasn't," Scott said. "Maybe he knew exactly what was going to happen."

"You know, maybe he did," Alice said. "So anyway, when he returned to the kitchen wrapped in the towel, Mrs. Jones said, 'Now isn't that better? I've made you a sandwich and some hot cocoa. It will help to warm you up while I put your things in the dryer.'

"Carter told me that after a few minutes he became really sleepy so Mrs. Jones suggested that he lie down for a bit. She said she'd wake him in a little while when his clothes were dry. He agreed, knowing that he would still have enough daylight to finish shoveling the driveway." Alice paused. "At least that was what he told me."

"I think he was fibbing just a bit."

"I think so too. Mrs. Jones led him to a bedroom and tucked him in under soft blankets. She shut the door and he fell asleep quickly."

Alice grinned. "Carter told me that he really fell asleep. Maybe he was just playing possum. Is that what you would have done, Scott?"

"I might have. Don't stop now, Sheherazade."

"He told me that he had no idea how long he had been asleep when the bed moved beneath him and he woke up. He turned and saw Mrs. Jones laying beside him. He started to get up but she gently pushed him back down and giggled. 'Is this the first time you've been in bed with a woman?' she asked. When he just blushed, she continued, 'You're a virgin? I never suspected.' She smiled at him. 'That's all right,' she said. 'I'm glad that you are.' Her hands parted his towel and slid down his smooth chest." Alice took a deep breath. "Can you picture all this, Scott?"

"Oh yes. I certainly can. Did your brother tell you more?"

"He told me that he started to breathe like he'd been running a race. 'Good,' Mrs. Jones said as she noticed the blankets sticking up below his waist. 'Very good. You won't be a stranger to sex much longer.'

"She parted the sides of her robe and said, 'Now look at me and touch me. Touch me anywhere you want.' He placed his hands on her face and started to caress her. When he tried to touch her large breasts, however, he became scared and froze. She took his hand, pressed it to one breast and said, softly, 'It's okay, Carter. It's really okay.'"

"Oh yes," Scott sighed. "I can see it all."

Alice smiled. "Her breasts were soft and smooth. Then she reached under the towel and gently held his dick in her hand as she started to slowly stroke it. My brother told me that he almost came right then, but he was afraid to.

"Mrs. Jones uncovered herself and removed her robe, all the while stroking his dick first with one hand, then the other. Carter stared at her and felt the heat rise in his face. 'You've never seen a naked woman or a pussy before, have you?'

"'No,' he said, 'I haven't.'

"'Well, just like my breasts, my pussy is soft and warm, but it can also get wet, Carter. All you have to do is touch and stroke it. Touch my pussy. It's okay, really it is.'

"So he touched it. Isn't that what you would have done, Scott?"

"I would have touched her all over."

"I'll bet you would have," Alice said. "My brother touched her pussy and it was soft just like she'd said it would be. 'Now,' Mrs. Jones said, 'take your finger and follow mine.' He watched as she put her finger inside her. Then she removed hers and nudged him, so he slid his finger into her. 'Now, Carter, move your finger back and forth.' He did and then she said, 'Yes. That's right. Keep it going until your finger and my cunt are sopping wet. Then comes the fun part.'

"'Fun part?' he whispered.

"'Yes, Carter. You're going to put your dick into my soft, warm pussy and gently move it back and forth.'

"Carter didn't think a woman like Mrs. Jones would actually let him but when he pulled his wet finger from her pussy, she was so wet. 'Why me?' he asked, puzzled and so excited.

"'I chose you because you're not like the other boys. You're sensitive and quiet. You keep to yourself.' She held his hot, hard dick then touched her pussy with the tip of it. He leaned toward her, dick throbbing so much it almost hurt. He closed his eyes so he could better feel what was happening. 'That's okay, Carter,' she said. 'Just feel.'

"Carter told me that Mrs. Jones's pussy was so warm and wet."

"I'll bet it was," Scott said.

"Mrs. Jones said, 'Your dick feels so good, all firm and warm and young.' She rubbed it over her wet pussy, then said, 'Now, Carter, push it all the way in.' He pushed gently but she said, 'Push harder. *Yesss*.'

"She pulled him so he was lying on top of her, his dick pushed into her cunt. My brother told me that he wanted to move but he didn't know whether he should. Should he, Scott?"

"Oh God, yes. Fuck her senseless, kid."

"Mrs. Jones said, 'Yes, Carter, move. Rock back and forth.'

"'Can I go faster?' he asked."

Scott's voice was hoarse as he said, "Go faster, kid. Fuck her hard."

"'You can,' she said, 'but since this is your first time, try to go slowly. See how nice it feels when you go slowly. We've got a long time.'

"'But your driveway . . .' "

"To hell with the driveway, Carter," Scott said, panting. "Do it."

"'It doesn't matter,' Mrs. Jones said. 'We can stay here as long as you like. Now move gently, slowly in and out.'

"'I gotta . . .' He didn't know what.

"'I know,' Mrs. Jones said. 'That's good, Carter. It means you're going to shoot. You'll lose your cherry and be a real man.' "

"'I'm gonna . . .' He did, didn't he, Scott?"

Alice heard rhythmic rustling noises through the phone. "Is he still fucking her," Scott gasped. "Young studs can come over and over. Tell me he's still fucking her."

"Oh, he is," Alice said. "His ass is pushing, driving his dick into her. He spurted, but he was hard again almost immediately. He just kept fucking her until he spurted again.

"'That was wonderful, Carter,' Mrs. Jones said, 'but now you've got to help me. I can come like that if you lick me.'"

"Oh God, do it, kid. Lick her pussy," Scott said.

"'I don't know how,' he said. He was so tired, but he wanted to do all the things that Mrs. Jones would let him do.

"'Of course you don't,' she said. 'I'll teach you. Now kneel between my legs.' He looked at her pussy, the hair all wet from his come. She smelled sweet and salty. He didn't know what to do but she put her fingers on her pussy. 'Lick here like I'm a piece of candy. Lick everywhere. You'll get the hang of it quickly. I just know you will.'

"He licked until he thought his dick would burst again. 'Can I put it in again?' he asked her.

"'In a minute,' she said, showing him where to lick more. 'And rub right here,' she said, putting her finger on the hard, swollen place. 'Yes,' she said. 'Like that.' And she was breathing hard. 'Yes,' she said again and he felt her body move and wet juice ran from her pussy. 'Now put it in again,' she said and he did. Didn't he, Scott?"

All Alice could hear was harsh breathing, then a shout. She just kept talking, waiting for Scott to tell her to stop.

"'Now, Carter, make me feel it,' Mrs. Jones said. This time Carter wasn't as scared so he could move and rub her at the same time. He thrust in and out, pulling it out and ramming himself in as far as he could. He came quickly but she didn't let him pull out. She held him tightly, rocking against him."

"Wow," Scott said, his breathing slower now. "That was quite a story. Did he go back another day?"

"My brother told me that it was just about dark when he left her house. 'Come back again tomorrow and you can finish all kinds of things,' she called after him. My brother went back lots of times that winter. He got quite an education."

"I'll be he did. Thanks for the story, Sheherazade," Scott said. "Can I call again next week?"

"Of course."

It was going to take a lot of writing time, but this was going to work out just fine. Just fine indeed.

Chapter 7

$\mathcal{A}$s the weeks passed Alice's business grew. She now had four steady clients and a few times Velvet had called and asked whether she could take a new customer. She was beginning to think of her income as real. A week earlier the Rutlandt Nursing Home had finally had a vacancy and her mother had been moved there. The older woman seemed happy, spending much of her day in a wheelchair in the sunny solarium with several other older residents.

One Thursday morning, both Alice and Betsy arrived at Dr. Tannenbaum's office early to catch up on some paperwork. As they updated files, Alice said, "Betsy, I have a strange problem that I need to talk to you about. I take these phone calls and that's great. The guys enjoy it and I can usually hear them climax, but it all leaves me a bit frustrated. With Larry away this week, weren't you . . . well, what do you do?"

"For someone who can talk a man to orgasm, you sure have a way with words. Don't you masturbate?"

Alice couldn't get the word out. She talked on the phone about all manner of sexual topics in graphic detail, but she couldn't bring herself to say the word *masturbate* when talking about herself. "No," she said softly.

"Ever?" Betsy said, her eyes wide.

"Not really," Alice whispered.

"Well, you should. The only way to learn about how a woman gets pleasure is to get pleasure yourself." Betsy smiled. "Let me ask you a very blunt question. Have you ever had an orgasm?"

Alice snapped out an answer. "Of course."

"That's what you tell all your other friends. This is me you're talking to. Now, think again. Have you ever had an orgasm?"

Alice sighed. "Okay, okay. You're right. I'm not really sure. Ralph wasn't the best lover that ever was. He was pretty much the stick-it-in-and-wiggle-it-around type."

Betsy guffawed. "You're impossible."

"I know," Alice said, smiling ruefully. "Seriously, all I've ever had was Ralph. I've never been with anyone else."

"Then it's time you found out. Think of it as research. It will make you so much better at entertaining your clients if you know what you're talking about."

"I guess you're right. I've been making up a lot of what I say, using stories and other people's experiences."

"So go home tonight, read a sexy story or make one up in your head and just do it. Touch where it feels good. You certainly know how, in graphic detail."

Alice blushed. "I guess I do."

That evening, Alice had a regular client named Marcus at eight and Vic called at nine. By quarter of ten, she had told two sexy stories, had two men climax on the phone with her, and she was very excited herself. Masturbate. There would never be a better time. *How can I do this?* she wondered. *It feels so awkward and so wrong. It's my body,* she told herself, *and I'm allowed to touch it if I want to. And I want to.*

She stripped out of her clothes, pulled on her Jets T-shirt and climbed between her cool sheets. Her nipples were erect and as she wiggled around in bed, they rubbed erotically against the front of the shirt. As she lay on her back, she placed one palm against her nipple, rubbing the nub against her hand. She pulled her hand back. "Stop being such a sissy," she said aloud. "You can make men quiver but you're embarrassed to touch your own body. It's yours after all." Hesitantly, Alice raised her hand again and rubbed her nipple. Small spikes of pleasure knifed through her body. She rubbed the other, feeling the rockets slice from her breasts to her belly.

She slid her hand beneath the shirt and touched her naked breasts. She played with the nipples, feeling the heady pleasure for the first time. Hands shaking, she reached lower and touched her pubic mound, sliding her fingers through the springy hair.

"Why am I so reluctant to do this?" she asked. She moved her fingers deeper and found the soft flesh that was now so wet. Slowly she explored, her fingers gliding through the thick lubricant. When she touched her swollen clit she felt a jolt of pleasure and, surprised by how strong it was, she touched again. She rubbed and pressed, finding places where the pleasure was greatest, but, although it felt wonderful, she found that no matter how much she stroked, she was unable to get over the precipice to what she knew would be her first real orgasm. She needed something inside of her. She looked furtively at her bedside table, then at the top of her dresser.

"What am I feeling so guilty about?" she asked, climbing out of bed. She opened her top dresser drawer and found an old lipstick. The tube was plastic and, she reasoned, should be the right shape. She grabbed a tissue and rubbed it all over the plastic, removing any dirt then, lipstick tube in hand, she returned to the bed. She rubbed her clit for a moment, then took the tube and stroked it around her wetness. Trembling, she pressed the tube against the opening of her vagina and felt the end slip inside. She held the tube tightly with one hand, and rubbed her clit with the other.

Suddenly she felt a tightening low in her belly and a sort of tickling and twitching in her pussy. It took only a moment for her inner spring to wind tighter, then explode. She gasped, colors whirling behind her closed eyes. Her entire body shook.

She gradually eased her rubbing and then she removed the tube from her cunt. "Holy shit," she said. "So that's what it's all about." Still panting, she wiped off the lipstick tube, then went into the bathroom and dried her pussy. "Holy shit."

For several more nights, after fevered storytelling, Alice touched her body, experimenting and quickly discovering what felt the best.

About a week after her first orgasm, when Betsy arrived, she put a brown envelope in the drawer where Alice kept her purse. "What's that?" Alice asked.

"It's something you need to look at. Call it research."

Alice pulled out the envelope and glanced at the catalog inside. "Shop till you drop," Betsy said as Alice stared at the catalog in her hand. "You need toys to play with to add to your stories."

As Alice turned to the first page of the publication, the outer door opened. She quickly replaced the catalog in the envelope and dropped it back into the drawer. She'd definitely look at it later. She'd seen a dildo that would certainly work better than a lipstick tube. Then turning, she said, "Good morning, Mrs. Grumbacher." She focused on the six-year-old trailing behind the woman. "And Tracey. How are you this morning? Are you ready to have your picture taken with Barney?"

"Only if I have no cavities," the little girl said, her chin pointed at the floor.

"Have you been brushing?"

"Oh yes," she said. "Mommy and Dr. Tannenbaum showed me how."

"Then I'm sure that your teeth will be in great shape."

The little girl smiled. "I think this one's a little loose," she said, pointing to her top tooth.

"Wow. That means you're getting older. We'll just let Dr. Tannenbaum look at it."

Mrs. Grumbacher finished hanging up her coat. "You're so good with her," she said to Alice. "She's always so nervous coming here, despite how nice the doctor is. But she cheers right up for you."

"I'm glad I can help," Alice said.

"You're such a people person."

Right. Oh, the people I deal with. Alice winked at Betsy.

That evening, Velvet called. "Alice," she said, "I have a new client and no one to give him to. You know what Fridays are like. He just wants the standard, not stories or anything. Would you like to give it a try?"

Alice thought about it. She'd been doing very well with her stories. Somehow, telling a story was different from straight phone sex. Less personal, somehow. However Velvet had been so good to her and she really wanted to help, and yet, she didn't want to disappoint anyone either. She took a deep breath. "Sure. I guess."

"Listen. Just roll with it. I've heard a lot about you from a few of your clients and I've gotten several calls from friends of theirs. You'll do fine."

Alice took a deep breath. "I certainly will. Put him through." She hung up and perched on the edge of the bed. It was like flying without a net or without a script. Of course, she often changed her prewritten stories to fit the needs of the man she was talking to and the stories seldom ended where her written material had, but she always had the safety of those pages to fall back on. Now she would be completely on her own.

Moments later the phone rang. She dropped her shoulders and lifted the receiver. "Hello?" she said, softly.

"Hi, Sherry," the voice at the other end of the phone said. "I'm Tim."

"Well, good evening, Tim. Are you feeling horny tonight?"

"That's why I called. I need you."

"Oh, baby," Alice said, "it's nice to be needed. Tell me what you need."

"I need to poke my hard cock into your sweet pussy."

"*Ohhh,*" Alice sighed. "That sounds really good. Are you in a real hurry? I usually like it slow. Would you like to touch me first?"

"Yes. I really would. Do you have big tits?"

Always big tits, Alice thought, considering her medium-size breasts. "Oh yes. I have real trouble finding bras large enough."

"What kind of bra are you wearing right now?" Tim asked.

"What would you like it to be?"

"I like the lacy ones so I can peek at your nipples. Are they big?"

"Yes, of course. Just listening to you has made them really hard. My bra is red, you know. Red satin, with small slits at the point of each cup so my hard nipples can just stick through. Can you see them? Close your eyes and see them reaching for you."

There was a long breath. "Yes. I can see them."

"I'm wearing red panties, too, small ones that barely cover my bush. I'm a redhead," she said, "so my pussy hair's deep auburn."

"Pinch your nipples for me," Tim said. "Make them really hard."

Alice was wearing a beige nylon bra, but she opened her robe and pinched her nipples, already hardening with erotic stimulation. "*Ohhh,*" she squealed. "That's nice." And it was. "Can I touch your cock too? Take off your pants so I can touch your prick."

There was a rustling and the squeak of bedsprings. "Okay. You can touch me."

"I'll touch it, but I'll have to use your hand. Wrap your fingers around it so I can feel how very hard it is."

There was another long sigh. "Are you wearing just your red bra and panties?"

"Well, I have red stockings with lacy tops that come up almost to my pussy, and red high-heeled shoes too."

"Rub the stockings and tell me how it feels."

Alice rubbed the inside of her thigh. "It feels smooth and cool to the touch. I can feel the heat pouring from my pussy too. Are we touching your cock?"

"Yes. I'm going to get some baby oil."

"Oh yes. Do that."

"Will you rub your pussy for me, through those red panties?"

"Will you be peeking? I don't know whether I can touch my pussy with anyone looking."

Tim laughed. "I won't peek, I promise. But I want you to really touch your pussy. Will you really do it for me?"

Alice reached down and touched the crotch of her beige nylon panties, lightly brushing the tip of her clit through the fabric. "Yes, I'm doing it."

"I love the feel of wet pussy," Tim said, "and the smell and the taste."

"How does your cock feel? Is it very hard?"

"It is, but I don't want to spurt until you do. Are you rubbing your pussy?"

"Yes," Alice said, finding to her surprise that she was very aroused. The muffled sensation of her fingers on her flesh, through the nylon, was delicious. "It feels really good and I'm getting really horny."

"Tell me exactly what you're doing and how it feels."

"I'm rubbing my clit through my bright-red panties. It feels hot and really good."

"Slide your fingers under the panties and feel your naked pussy. I want to see you doing that while I rub my cock."

Alice slipped her fingers beneath the waistband of her panties, down through her pubic hair to her sopping cunt. She was so wet. From her few sessions, she knew where to touch so it felt best. "You know, this makes me so hungry for a cock inside of me. What should I do?"

"Get something and fill your snatch. Stuff it full and pretend that it's my big cock."

"I've got a big dildo and I'm putting it into my pussy." Alice propped the phone against her ear, reached for the lipstick tube and pressed in into her pussy. It wasn't enough. She wanted something bigger, something that would really fill her up. Something she could fuck herself with without being afraid of it slipping all the way inside. She flashed on the catalog Betsy had given her, then Tim said, "Is your snatch full?"

"Oh, I wish it were your cock that was filling me up. I'd wrap my legs around your waist and jam that cock deep into my pussy."

"Oh, Sherry," Tim groaned. "I'd drive into you so hard that you'd scream. I'd pound harder and harder."

Alice rubbed her clit through her panties while the lipstick tube rubbed the walls of her pussy. She felt her orgasm building. "You're going to make me come, Tim," she said. "Does your big cock feel good inside of me?"

"I'm fucking you so hard." She heard his rasping breaths and his moans.

"Yes, baby," she said as the orgasm flowed from her pussy to her thighs and her belly. She curled her toes and her breath caught in her throat. "I'm coming. Yes," she gasped.

"Oh, Sherry. I came all over the bed."

"I came too," she said, surprise obvious in her voice.

"That makes it so much better somehow. Thanks, Sherry."

"You're welcome, I'm sure. I hope you'll call again."

"Maybe. My wife's away and I just needed something."

"I hope to hear from you the next time your wife's away."

"Yeah," Tim said, and she heard the click as he hung up the phone. Alice grinned and slowly stood up, pulled off her clothes and climbed between the sheets, naked tonight. As Roger curled up against her side, Alice looked at the blue denim drapes she had made for the bedroom when she and Ralph had first moved into the apartment. "You know, Roger, I think I'll get some new drapes. And maybe a matching bedspread." She reached over, turned off the light and was asleep instantly.

One Thursday morning a few weeks later, Betsy arrived at work. It was the second week in May and everyone was in a great mood. "I've got a plan," she said to Alice. "I called Velvet last night and she's free this evening. Larry's taking the boys to see *Friday the Thirteenth, Part Seventy-six, Jason Runs for Congress*, or something like that, so I'm off the hook too. I thought we'd all have a girls' night out, just the three of us, maybe at Patches. Silly drinks with lots of orange juice, rum, and those little umbrellas. How about it? Got any calls tonight?"

"No. I've settled on Mondays, Wednesdays, and Fridays."

"Great. We're meeting at Patches at seven."

"I really should get down to Rutlandt and see Mom. I haven't been there since the weekend."

"Come on, babe. You need some time for just you. You

work here five days a week, you take calls three nights, you visit your mom each weekend and at least once during the week. Take some time off."

Alice leaned back in her chair. "Maybe it would be all right. God it sounds nice."

"Great. I'm counting on you. Seven at Patches."

At just past seven, Alice arrived at Patches, a restaurant and watering hole at one end of a long enclosed mall. The place was crowded with couples with small children enjoying overstuffed sandwiches and fries, teens sharing secrets and stuffed potato skins, and businessmen in suits and ties downing a few drinks before going home. Servers of both sexes wandered between the tables, dressed in outrageous outfits, tight white T-shirts and black jeans, both covered with squares of brightly patterned fabric.

Alice looked around and found Betsy and Velvet sitting at a small table off to one side. As Alice approached the table, Velvet stood up and embraced her lightly, kissing her on each cheek. "I'm so glad this worked out. I've been meaning to get together with you."

"Yes," Betsy said. "I was afraid you'd changed your mind and gone to visit your mom after all."

"I decided I needed some time out," Alice said as she dropped into a chair. She looked at the tall glasses filled with orange liquid that stood in front of each woman. "What are those?"

"Those," Velvet said, "are Bahama Mamas: rum, pineapple juice, coconut liqueur, and heaven knows what else. They are delicious." She lifted her glass and took a long drink through the straw.

Their waitress arrived and Alice considered ordering a diet soda, then changed her mind. "I'll have one of those," she said, pointing to the tall golden drinks.

"One Bahama Mama," the waitress said, scribbling on her order pad. "Any munchies for you ladies? The buffalo wings are terrific tonight and so are the skins."

Betsy tipped her head to one side, then said, "Why not? One of each. We only live once and to hell with the calories."

"I'll bring them right over."

Velvet leaned toward Alice. "You are really quite something," she said. "You've taken to this so quickly. The men I talk to when I route the calls rave about you. They feel they know you personally, particularly about all your daring exploits."

Alice grinned. "Thanks. It's really gotten to be fun."

"Betsy's an old hand at this, so I don't have to tell her how terrific she is now," Velvet said, patting Betsy on the hand, "but she took several months to get into the swing of it all. You've developed quite a following in the few weeks you've been doing it."

"I like my guys," Alice said. "They are really nice people. There are a few losers, of course, but most of them are just lonely men who want a warm voice with a lurid story to tell. I fit the bill."

"The men really surprised me when I first started working the phone," Betsy said. "I expected maniacs, kinky guys who wanted bizarre stuff with lots of sweaty sex but most of them are just ordinary men who want bizarre stuff and lots of sweaty sex."

The three women laughed, all sharing the same feelings. "How did you get time off this evening?" Alice asked Velvet.

"I've got another woman working the routing tonight. She's been doing it a few nights a week and it's great for me to get some time off."

The three women talked for an hour, sipping several rounds of drinks and munching on wings and skins. "Has he got the greatest buns or what?" Betsy said, gazing at one of the waiters who walked past them in his almost obscenely tight jeans.

Alice looked at the young man and sighed. "He's got a

really great body. Remember that bulge in the front of Mr. Hollingsworth's pants?"

"Who could forget?" Betsy told Velvet about their high school social studies teacher.

"Maybe I'll use him in one of my stories," Alice said. "High school teacher and unruly student."

"How about him?" Velvet said, indicating a man sitting in the corner, watching the people and sipping a glass of red wine. "That's my style."

Alice turned and looked at the man Velvet had indicated. He was in his mid-thirties, with long black hair caught in a thin, black leather thong at the base of his neck. He wore a tight black turtleneck shirt and black trousers. "There's something both attractively compelling and dangerous about him," Velvet said. "That's the stuff of my fantasies."

"Umm. I love a little danger," Betsy said.

"I'd love a little anything," Alice said, then slammed her mouth shut.

Betsy turned to her. "What does that mean?"

"Sorry. Just my big mouth and one too many Bahama Mamas. It's nothing."

"No, it's not nothing. Don't tell me you've finally decided that it's time to get out into the world." Betsy leaned toward Velvet. "She hasn't really dated since her husband split on her."

"I have too. You've set me up with lots of guys."

"Yeah. Right. You meet them at my house, have maybe one date, then nothing."

"You're kidding," Velvet said. "I would have thought you had a rich and varied dating life, from what your fans tell me."

"My fans. Guys who have no clue who I am. They all think I'm some kind of swinger with an exotic past and a spectacular future." Alice realized that she was just a bit tipsy and willing to talk about her lack of a social life. "I'm starting to think I've missed the boat. You two are married, you've got kids. Me? I play on the phone three nights a week and otherwise, nothing."

"So why don't you do something about it?"

"Like what?" Alice sipped her drink to keep the slight buzz that was allowing her to talk about herself so freely.

"Like date," Velvet said.

"Excuse me. I don't seem to see the line of nice guys queuing up to take me out. I don't know a soul except you two and the guys on the phone, and I couldn't consider them as date material."

"Why not?" Betsy chimed in. "You just finished saying that most of them are really just nice, lonely guys. Haven't any of them asked to meet you in person?"

Alice thought about Vic, her first and steadiest client. "Sure. Remember Vic, Velvet? The first guy you put me on with? He's a decent guy, lonely and alone. At least that's what he tells me. He asks me out almost every time we talk."

"So?" the two other women said in unison. "Does he live around here?"

"He lives in the city, but get real. He thinks I'm a sexual sophisticate, with blond hair and big. . ." She looked down at the front of her green blouse. "Anyway. He has no clue what Alice is like. He likes Sheherazade." She lowered to her phone voice. "Woman of the world."

"So meet some businessman who doesn't know you from Eve," Betsy said. "Go out. Have a blast."

"Where would you suggest I meet this Mr. Business? I'm not the type to sit at a bar and wait for some guy to ask me what my sign is."

Velvet sipped her drink. "I've got several single male friends, one in particular I think you'd like. If you wouldn't object, I could introduce you. I'd give him your phone number."

Alice giggled. "You're pretty good at occupying my phone."

"So," Betsy added, "why don't you let one of your phone friends take you out. What have you got to lose?"

"A client," Alice said.

"Bullshit," Velvet said. "You could have more clients than you know what to do with. Pick one who sounds nice and go for it."

"These guys will expect Sheherazade, not Alice."

"Next time someone asks you out, take some time and tell him who you are." Velvet continued, "Call him off-line and just talk."

"I couldn't do that. He'd never believe me again."

"I'm sure that only a few of the men believe you now," Velvet said. "You don't think that these guys think you've actually done all the things you tell them about, do you? They're into the fantasy. They close their eyes and live those experiences with you. They know you're making it all up but it just doesn't matter."

"Like this Vic," Betsy said. "Let him learn who the real you is and he won't be nearly as surprised as you think."

Alice giggled. "Are you two ganging up on me?"

"Yes, we are," Betsy said. "I've been trying to get you out of your shell for years. Now that I've got the chance, I'm using all the help I can get." She reached across the table and, with an exaggerated movement, shook Velvet's hand. "This is a campaign to get Alice out into the big, wide world. Right, general?"

"Right, admiral," Velvet said. "And you, private, are taking orders. Do it. Soon."

"Private," Alice said, laughing. "I'm about the most public private that ever was."

Later that night, Alice crawled into bed beside Roger. "What do you think, cat?" she said. "Are Betsy and Velvet right? Am I still the spinster type despite Sheherazade?"

Roger rolled over and allowed Alice to scratch his belly. "Right. You agree with them. Well, if the opportunity presents itself, maybe . . . I'll think about it."

Merrow.

Chapter 8

The following Monday evening, Vic called. "Hi, Sherry," he said. "Got a story for me tonight?"

"Sure thing, sweet cheeks," Alice said in her Sheherazade voice. "It's about a night when I was very naughty."

"Tell me."

"Well, you know I was married a long time ago."

"Yes. I remember."

"Well it happened back then." She thought about the story she had written about a game of strip poker. She couldn't think of Ralph ever playing like this so she decided to rename her husband. "Ted and I had met this other couple, Barb and Andy, the day after they moved in next door to us. Nice folks and we hit it off right away. It hadn't hurt that Andy was quite a hunk. He wasn't actually gorgeous, but he had great eyes and the best pair of buns I had ever seen."

"Women always like buns, don't they?"

"Actually, what appeals to me now is a nice personality and

a good sense of humor, but back then I was really into looks."

"I think I've got good buns, but only a woman would know for sure."

"I'll bet you have great buns, Vic." Alice was amazed. She was actually flirting with Vic. Back to work.

"The four of us had found ourselves meeting often beside the pool in the center of the condo complex. Friday evenings we were all tired from work and sat in the water, talking about everything from our jobs to television to sports to religion, politics and, of course, sex. As the summer wore on, we started to bring potluck suppers out to the pool area. As fall approached and we had to give up the pool, we started to alternate Friday dinners at each other's houses, and eventually Ted and I succumbed to Barb and Andy's shared love of poker.

"It started with matchsticks, then chips, and eventually we began to play for small change. We won and lost a few dollars and we put the winnings into a kitty to take us all out to an expensive restaurant."

"I like an occasional game of poker but I'm not very good," Vic said. "I can't bluff worth a damn. You can tell exactly what I'm thinking by just looking at my face."

"Me too. I'm hopeless."

"That's good. Go on with the story."

"Well, one night Barb had lost five dollars, the maximum amount allowed by our house rules. 'Okay,' she said, as Ted raked in the pile of coins from the center of the table, 'I'm tapped.' She wiggled her eyebrows. 'What shall I wager now?'

"I just stared. Her suggestion was obvious but I thought that she must be teasing. 'I'll ante for you,' I said, pushing a nickel into the center of the table."

"You were really embarrassed?" Vic asked.

"Yeah, I was." Alice smiled. "I wasn't always the sexually sophisticated woman I am now."

Softly, Vic asked, "Are you really so sophisticated or just a good storyteller?"

Alice gasped. Did he know her that well? Without answering, she continued her story. "Barb thanked me but looked a bit disappointed.

"'Rats,' my husband said. 'I was hoping for something better.' I playfully slapped him on the back of the hand. 'Not a chance, buster.'

"He laughed. 'Rats, I say again.'

"Andy, Barb's husband, dealt seven-card stud. In deference to Barb, the betting was small and we allowed her to stay in despite her continued losses. Soon she had a small pile of coins in front of her to keep track of her indebtedness. 'I'll bet a nickel. I'll win this one for sure,' she said, grinning at her cards. 'Whatever would I do if I lost?'

"'Call,' Ted said.

"'I'll call too,' I said, hoping that Barb would win and the game could continue without the double meanings that seemed to pepper the conversation now. I was really embarrassed.

"Andy called and said, 'Time to show what you've got— cards, that is.'

"'Full boat, tens over threes,' Ted said. I was sure my husband had won and confused as to what would happen then. Andy and I turned our cards face down, signaling that we couldn't beat Ted's hand. 'And you, my indebted friend?' Ted said.

"'Shit,' Barb hissed, 'I really thought I had you. I have a flush, queen high.'

"'Phew,' Andy said. 'I haven't had a hand as good as either of those all night. Ted, since you're the winner, you get to decide Barb's payment.'"

"What did he ask for?" Vic asked.

"He asked her to take off her blouse. I was shocked at my husband, but I said nothing. I was sure that Barb would be insulted and I was afraid that our wonderful Friday evenings were suddenly gone. I'll have to admit, Vic, that I was also aroused."

"I'll bet," Vic said.

"'You've got it,' Barb said, and with little hesitation, she unbuttoned her shirt and pulled it off. I kept my gaze on the coins in front of me, then slowly raised my eyes. Barb was an average-looking woman with a nice figure, shoulder-length brown hair, and green eyes covered with glasses. As I looked up, I saw her medium-size breasts, now covered only by a wispy bit of white lace. I swallowed hard, then glanced at Ted. He was looking at Barb's body, but I felt his fingers link with mine. He glanced at me and squeezed my hand.

"'I love those sexy things my wife wears,' Andy said, 'don't you?'

"'I guess,' I said. Actually Barb wasn't wearing much less than she often wore at the pool but this was so much more intimate. I could see the outline of her nipples through the sheer fabric and I was sure that the men could too.

"Andy reached over and rubbed his palm over the tips of Barb's breasts. 'God, she has great tits.' I watched Andy's hand, unable to look away.

"'Okay, that's enough,' Barb quipped. 'Let's deal.'

"It was my turn to deal and, with shaking hands, I picked up the cards and shuffled, staring at the table. 'Hey, Sherry,' Barb said, placing her hand over mine, 'I didn't mean to embarrass you. I'm really sorry. I wouldn't hurt you for the world.' She reached for her shirt and stuffed one arm into a sleeve.

"'Of course not,' the men said.

"I sighed. 'I guess I'm just a bit more of a prude than you all are.'

"'Not in bed you're not,' my husband said. 'This woman's a wildcat under the right circumstances.'

"I could feel the heat rise in my face. I loved good hot sex, but up till then I had been very private about it. Yet here my husband was, telling everyone. He was such a beast. Or was he? Was there any reason to be so afraid to let anyone know that I enjoyed good lovemaking?"

"No reason at all," Vic purred. "Do you enjoy good lovemaking now, Sherry?"

Suddenly breathless, Alice said, "Yes. I guess so."

"Do you get enough?"

"Let's get back to the story. Okay?"

"Sure," Vic said, but Alice thought she heard reluctance in his voice. "Tell me more."

"Well, I was chagrined. I wasn't a prude and I knew I had to lighten up. These were my best friends. 'Listen,' I said, 'leave the shirt off. You lost fair and square. But you'll win this hand for sure.'

"Barb did win that hand and a few more and by the end of the evening, everything was the same as it had been. After Barb and Andy were gone, I found that the thought of Barb without her shirt had me terribly turned on. Ted and I cavorted on the bed for almost an hour. Finally we lay side by side, hands clasped, our breathing slowing. 'You found that bit with Barb's blouse a turn-on, didn't you?' Ted asked.

"I thought about the answer for a minute, then said, 'I didn't think so at the time, but I guess I did. The sight of her in that bra and watching Andy's hand rubbing her made me hot.'

"'Yeah, me too,' Ted said. 'Not the sight of her tits, but watching Andy touch her. God, it made me hard as stone. It's not personal, you understand,' he continued. 'It doesn't mean I love you any less.'

"'I know that,' I said, and I did know that. I knew he loved me, but the sight of a half-naked body was a turn-on. Nothing more was said, but I lay awake for quite a while that evening.

"The following week we were at Andy and Barb's house and after dinner we moved to the card table. As the play began, Ted cleared his throat and broached the topic we were all a bit afraid of. 'I say that we cut the maximum loss to a dollar. I liked what happened last week when Barb got tapped out.'

"'I have to say that sex was great that night,' Andy said. 'Watching my wife revealed for all to see made me really hot.'

"'Dollar losses?' Ted said. He looked at me. 'Okay, babe?'

"I found my head nodding. Soon I was down my limit and then some. 'Shirt please,' Andy said."

"Could you do it?" Vic asked. "I mean just like that?"

"I didn't think about it, I just did it."

"I'll bet you have a great body."

Alice sighed. "I guess every woman wishes she had a better one."

"Every man too. Go on with your story."

"I had worn my sexiest black lace bra under my sweat-shirt. I guess I had known what would happen and the whole idea really turned me on. 'God,' Andy said, 'you've got a great body.' I never thought of myself as having a good shape, but, as my face got hotter I looked at Andy. He had the most wonderful look in his eyes.

"Over the next half hour, Barb was clearly the big winner and had almost all the coins in front of her. I had almost become used to sitting at the table in only my bra. When Andy was tapped, Barb said, 'Listen, losing shirts isn't as revealing for you guys as it is for us. I demand your jeans.' I remember thinking, *God, she is a daring one.*

"I swallowed, wondering whether I would get to see those gorgeous buns covered only by a pair of shorts. Andy agreed and quickly removed his jeans. He was wearing the smallest pair of briefs I had ever seen and they barely covered the bulge caused by his obvious erection. As he sat down, he said, 'As you can obviously tell, this has gone a bit further than before. Let me be honest with you two. Barb and I have been talking. Before we moved here, we had a pair of friends and we all used to play together on occasion. No one actually did it with anyone else's husband or wife, but there was a lot of fooling around and a few times we each made love with the other couple watching. It was a great turn-on.'

"I remember how shocked I was. 'You didn't,' I said, horrified yet also soaking wet.

"'Yes, we did,' Barb said. 'We never actually swapped, but it was so hot to play and to watch. We touched one another with hands and mouth and it was incredibly exciting. We wouldn't jeopardize our friendship by asking anything you two weren't willing to do but that bra you're wearing, Sherry, says a lot.'

"'It does?' I said, trying not to sound anxious. My mouth was dry and my hands trembled.

"'I think you wore it on purpose, hoping this would happen,' Barb said.

"Ted grinned at me. 'That's what I thought when I saw you dressing, and that's why I suggested what I did.' "

"Did you 'fess up, Sherry?" Vic asked. "Had you done it on purpose?"

Alice chuckled as she looked at the story she had written. "I admitted it."

"'Have you ever played with another couple before?' Barb asked.

"'Never,' Ted said. 'We'd never even considered it until last Friday night. After you guys left we had some of the hottest sex I can remember, and I must admit that I was thinking about the sight of your body and of Andy touching you.'

"'Me too,' I whispered.

"Andy stood up and quickly slipped Barb's sweater over her head, revealing another tiny bra and her gorgeous breasts. 'Let's all get more comfortable,' he suggested, removing his sweatshirt, shoes, and socks. Barb stood, slipped out of her shoes and pulled off her jeans. She was wearing a pair of bikini panties that barely covered her mound. Ted took a deep breath, and said to me, 'Babe? Is this all right with you? If it's not we can stop now.'"

"Was it okay with you?" Vic asked, clearly excited by the picture Alice was painting.

"In answer, I stood up and pulled off my jeans. Like Barb I had worn a pair of tiny bikini panties.

"'You really are gorgeous,' Andy said. I knew better. I had a not-bad body with a little extra flesh here and there, but the look on Andy's face said that he thought I was wonderful and that made my knees turn to jelly.

"My husband was the last to strip. When he was finally down to a pair of tight briefs, I stared, then giggled. 'Those are new. I'll bet you bought those special, thinking something like this might happen.'

"'Busted,' he said. 'Last Friday made me so hot, I was just hoping.' Suddenly everyone was laughing, and moving into the living room. Standing in the middle of the room, Ted placed his lips against mine and kissed me long and deeply. His hands roamed over my back, cupped my ass, and caressed my calves. Calves? My eyes sprung open. Andy sat at my feet, his hands stroking my legs. At first I stiffened, but then I relaxed and enjoyed the feeling of someone else's hands on my body. Slowly his hands slid to the fronts of my thighs, then quieted. 'I can feel you tremble,' he said softly. 'Are you afraid? Has this gone too far?'

"'No,' I whispered. 'It all feels good.'"

"I wish I had been there," Vic said. "I'd love to touch you."

"I wish you had been too," Alice said, realizing that as she told the story, she thought about Vic. "So Barb moved behind Ted, her palms flat on his upper back. Then she turned my husband so he was facing her and she gazed into my eyes. 'If this bothers you,' she said to me, 'I'll stop.' When I didn't say anything, she slipped her arms around Ted's neck and pressed her lips against his.

"*I should make them stop,* I remember saying to myself.

Another woman's kissing my husband. But it was so sexy. As I watched, Barb rubbed her lace-covered breasts over Ted's chest. *Funny,* I said to myself, *I'm not really jealous. It's really erotic watching my husband enjoy what's happening.* And he was. His arms were around Barb and he was kissing her with the same mouth that had just been against my lips and it was all right. I knew that this wasn't going to go too far, and I could call it off at any time. But I didn't want to.

"Suddenly Andy's hands were on my naked belly, stroking, caressing, kneading. He stood up and his hands slid to my ribs. 'May I? I want so much to touch you.'"

Alice could hear Vic groan.

"I looked into his deep brown eyes, smiled, and touched his face. 'Yes,' I whispered. 'It really is all right.'

"His hands were on my breasts, cupping me, feeling the weight of my tits in his palms. His fingers found my nipples through the silky fabric and he pinched. 'Oh God,' I said as my eyes closed and my knees buckled."

"Oh God," Vic moaned.

"Quickly Andy guided me to the sofa. As I lay back on the soft material, I knew that nothing else mattered but hands and mouths and satisfying the rising tide of heat. Andy crouched between my spread thighs and his mouth found my nipples. Then his teeth. That had always been my downfall. The slight pain on my nipples drove me crazy. I held his head as he nipped and nibbled, moisture flowing between my legs, soaking the crotch of my panties. I ran my fingers through his curly hair, so unlike Ted's straight soft hair. This wasn't my husband, but it was so good.

"Suddenly there was a mouth on my other breast. My eyes flew open and I saw Ted's head bent over me. I had a mouth on each breast and Barb stood behind, stroking each man's back.

"Ted unsnapped the front hook of my bra and now

mouths engulfed naked nipples. Sharp teeth. Pinching fingers. A hand stroked me between my thighs. Ted's? Andy's? I found I didn't want to know so I closed my eyes.

"Fingers rubbed through the silk of my panties. My clit swelled to press against those hands. Fingers slipped under the edge of my panties and found my wetness. Fingers slowly found my center and one penetrated just a tiny bit. Not enough, my body cried as I thrust my hips upward. Fill me.

"Hands removed my panties and still my eyes remained closed. I wanted to imagine that they were Andy's fingers, not my husband's. Then the fingers filled me, first one, then two, then three, filling my emptiness. I drove my hips upward, forcing the fingers to fill me more deeply. I had to know.

"I opened my eyes. Ted was on his hands and knees, his head bent over my breast. Barb had one hand on the small of his back, the other obviously rubbing him between his thighs. Andy was between my legs, one hand buried in my pussy, the other stroking his now-naked cock."

"I'm going to come, Sherry," Vic cried.

Alice knew that the best way for him to get off was for her to continue the story. "Then Andy's mouth found my clit, his tongue ceaseless in its exploration, his fingers still filling me. It was too much and I came. Waves and waves of molten heat washed over me and I heard myself screaming. As I climaxed, Andy straightened and I watched a stream of come arch from his cock onto my belly. As I calmed, Ted and Barb pulled off their remaining clothing and Barb lay on the carpet. Ted bent between her legs and pressed his mouth over her clit.

"I was now almost unconscious on the couch so Andy slid to the floor and sat beside me. He reached out, laid a hand on his wife's arm and spoke softly to me. 'You've never felt anything like touching your husband while he makes love like this. Touch him.'

"Hesitantly I reached out and placed my hand on my

husband's back. I could feel the movements of his body as he licked Barb's pussy. 'If you're up to it,' Andy whispered, 'come here and touch him right.' He pulled my hand and, although I was exhausted from my own climax, I moved onto the floor until I could reach between his thighs and place my hand on Ted's cock. He was hard and hot and so smooth. I squeezed and felt his entire body tighten.

"I smiled and stroked him the way I knew he liked as I watched his head bob between Barb's thighs. I rubbed and squeezed until I knew he was getting close. I kept him there, on the edge of climax until I heard Barb scream, then I took one finger and scratched the special spot between his ass and his balls. He came, his come spurting onto Barb's thigh."

"Oh God, yes," Vic cried, his voice relaxing.

"Except for the sound of heavy breathing, the room was silent for a while. Then Ted said, 'I need a shower. Do you think there's room for four?' "

"Oh, Sherry," Vic said, his breathing slowing, "that was wonderful."

"I'm glad you enjoyed my story. It happened a long time ago."

"Did it really happen?"

"Of course."

Vic's voice got serious. "Really? Sherry, tell me about you. Are you really the woman you seem to be?"

Alice hesitated. She really liked Vic. Although she hardly knew him, she sensed that he was really lonely. "Some parts of me are, some aren't."

"We've been teasing for weeks. I ask you out and you change the subject. Let me ask again. I already know that we only live about fifty miles apart. So how about meeting me for dinner some evening? I could come up from the city and we could meet somewhere in Westchester."

"I'm not the woman you think I am, you know."

"I don't know what I think you are but I'll bet you don't

look at all like the picture I have of you."

"Not at all."

"Long blond hair? Blue eyes?"

"Brown curly hair, brown eyes. About five-three."

"Are you married? Living with someone?"

"No. I'm alone." Why had she said it quite that way?

"Listen. I've been calling sex lines for a long time and somehow you and I have some things in common. You sound like a nice person and maybe a bit lonely like me. I know a nice informal restaurant in northern Westchester." He mentioned a place called Donovan's in Mount Kisco, a twenty-minute drive from her house.

"I know the place."

"What nights do you work?"

"Mondays, Wednesdays, and Fridays."

"Okay. Saturday sounds too much like a date and this isn't. Just two friends meeting for dinner. Let's make it next Tuesday. I'll be at Donovan's at seven. I'll get a table and sit with a copy of Shakespeare's sonnets. It's hokey, but who else would have such a book. I'm thirty-eight and not much to look at so you might see me and decide to run for the hills." His laugh was self-deprecating, but warm. "I'll wait until seven-thirty, then order dinner and eat slowly. Please come."

He was so sweet and thoughtful. "I don't know."

"I don't either. I'll just hope. Okay?"

"Okay, but don't expect anything. I might not be there."

"I know. Good night, Sherry. Oh. Is that your real name?"

Alice sighed. "It's Alice. Alice Waterman. And I'm thirty-two and not much to look at either."

"Nice to meet you, Alice. I'm Vic Sanderson."

The following Thursday evening the three women met again at Patches for girls' night out. Besides Betsy, Alice had never had a good female friend and the more time she spent with Velvet, the more comfortable and the closer she felt.

The three women had arrived at six-thirty and had decided to try Caribbean Romances: pineapple juice, orange juice, rum, and amaretto. After one drink and lots of small talk, Alice broached the topic that had been troubling her since her conversation with Vic.

"I've got a problem," she said without preamble. "Vic asked me out again."

"And?"

"And I don't know what to do."

"What do you want to do?" Velvet asked.

Alice chuckled. "It depends on what time of day you ask. Sometimes I tell myself that he's a lonely, sensitive man who seems to like me. The rest of the time I think he's a man who has no clue who I am and who likes to call phone-sex lines."

"Did you make a date?"

Alice filled them in on Vic's arrangement. "Sounds sensible," Velvet said, understanding that Alice didn't want a flip answer. "Each of you has a car so you have a way out if it all goes wrong. No one knows enough about the other to be troublesome. It sounds like a good plan to me."

"I guess he must have given it quite a bit of thought," Alice admitted.

"He's obviously been planning this for quite a while," Velvet added.

"Okay," Betsy said, "let's look at this seriously. What's the downside?"

Alice considered. "He's expecting Sherry, girl sexpot. Someone who's been with everyone and done everything. And what will he get? Me."

"Do you think he wants sex with you? Right there in Donovan's?"

"No, of course not."

"Right. You'll just talk, have a nice dinner, and get to know each other. I repeat, what's the downside?"

Alice smiled ruefully. "I don't know. It just so embarrassing to have to admit that I'm not what he thinks I am."

Velvet leaned forward. "You know he doesn't believe all that sexy stuff you tell him over the phone. He knows you're not Sheherazade. Maybe he wouldn't be interested if he thought you were."

"What do you mean?"

"He's a small, lonely man who's probably never actually made love to a woman like Sherry. Maybe the idea of dating her would scare him to death. It would be like making love to some porn star, a constant judge of his technique."

"She's right, you know," Betsy said. "Most of the men I talk to aren't the worldly type who would enjoy being with the woman I pretend to be. They'd probably enjoy fucking my brains out as long as they didn't have to watch my eyes or talk to me afterward." She paused. "I'm probably pretty threatening. Maybe if they could say, 'Down on your knees, bitch,' then make me disappear."

"I never thought of it that way," Alice said.

"I don't know," Velvet said. "I've never dated any of my clients, but then I've been married the entire time and I wouldn't have even considered it."

"So we're back to the question of what's the downside," Betsy said.

Alice grinned. "I don't know. Maybe there isn't one." With two Caribbean Romances making her feel a bit mellow, Alice had to admit that if she showed up at Donovan's the following Tuesday, she had very little to lose.

Chapter 9

$\mathcal{A}$lice was almost useless at Dr. Tannenbaum's office on Tuesday. At unexpected moments she'd drift off into a fantasy about her dinner date with Vic. In one, she walked into the restaurant and was greeted by a hunky guy dressed in a tuxedo, and in another he was dressed in a gorilla suit. In another dream, they sat, had dinner, and then Vic asked her to climb under that table and suck his cock. None of the dreams left her feeling comfortable.

"So what are you going to wear?" Betsy said, dropping into a chair in the reception area.

"Huh?" Alice said, returning from a vision of the two of them in a heart-shaped, vibrating bed.

"Tonight. What are you wearing?"

"I've decided not to go."

"You're crazy. At least go to Donovan's and see what he looks like. If he scares the daylights out of you, turn around, and walk out. Give it a chance."

"Why? He'll just be disappointed and I'll feel terrible."

"Both Velvet and I tried to convince you that he won't be disappointed. I think he's very perceptive to be able to see the wonderful woman you are. I'm sure it comes through in your stories. You're always considerate and thoughtful and you're such a caring person."

"Thanks for that. This whole thing's making me crazy."

"Okay. Here's what you do. Go home after work, put on those new gray linen slacks and your soft mauve silk blouse, the one you bought a few weeks ago at Macy's."

"I don't know."

"I do. Wear a pair of chunky silver earrings and that silver chain with the disk at the end." Betsy stopped to think. "Let's see. I've got the rest. Your deep burgundy wool vest in case it's chilly, and your trench coat. See? Nothing more to think about."

"But . . ."

"Enough of the buts. Just do it because Betsy says so. End of thought."

"Yes, Betsy," Alice said in a little-girl voice.

"That's a good girl," Betsy said, smiling. "You only have to walk into Donovan's and look. Then I give you permission to turn around and walk out. Okay?"

"Okay. I'll do it."

"We'll meet for lunch tomorrow so I can hear everything, good or bad."

After she and Betsy arranged their lunch, Alice hurried home from work, both exhilarated and terrified. She showered and dressed as Betsy had suggested and at seven-ten she was parked in the lot at Donovan's. She got out of her car and approached the green and white striped awning. The restaurant was American-style, the entire place decorated to resemble someone's patio, with white walls, white slatted wood tables, green and white striped chairs, table cloths, and napkins. At first look, it was blinding and it felt like being inside of a lime candy cane but it was all softened by the dozens of green plants that filled white pots throughout the dining room. The restaurant was extremely popular with well-priced dishes and a list of specials that took up half of one wall.

As she wandered toward the host, a woman offered to take her coat. "No thanks. I might not be staying." She stood at the entrance to the huge dining room and looked around. She saw a few single men, but finally her eyes rested upon a middle-aged man with a copy of Shakespeare on the table in front of him. He had shaggy brown hair, deep brown eyes, and deep laugh lines around his mouth. Alice saw that his ears were oversized, which was probably why he wore his hair long. She smiled. *He looks like a basset hound,* she thought, *comfortable somehow.* She squared her shoulders and walked into the room. The host approached and asked whether she needed a table. "No thanks, I'm meeting someone."

Vic caught her eye and when she nodded, his face lit up. He stood as she neared his table and quickly the host pulled out a chair for her. Vic was several inches taller than she was, maybe five foot eight or nine. "I'm so glad you could come," Vic said. He extended his hand and she took it briefly. His palm was warm and a bit damp, his hands soft.

"I almost didn't," Alice said, releasing his hand and settling in her chair.

"If you want the truth, I almost didn't show up either."

"How come?" Alice asked, handing her coat to the host. "Could you put this in the checkroom for me?" she asked him. She'd stay for a while at least.

"Of course," the host said, bustling away.

"All day I had these visions of you," Vic admitted, "looking like one of those Baywatch women with long legs and a big bosom. You'd take one look at me and run for the hills."

Alice laughed. "I had the same thoughts. Funny. You don't look like Hulk Hogan in a suit."

The two laughed together. "My ex-wife used to say that I looked like a basset hound with big friendly eyes."

"No," Alice said, trying to hide her chuckle. "I think you look just fine. It was so nice of you to drive all the way up here."

"Actually I love driving and I do a lot of it, usually by myself to get away and think."

They ordered a house-special chicken dish with baked potatoes and broccoli and throughout dinner the two talked like they were old friends. It turned out that they were both New York Jets fans and they talked at length about the team's prospects for the coming season. They also liked folk music. Vic raved about a small fifty-seat auditorium in Greenwich Village where they had unusual groups perform each weekend. "A few weeks ago they had a really wonderful group of Andean musicians. They played some fantastic stuff on the charango, guitar, and bombo."

"I have an album of Andean music that I particularly enjoy. Isn't one of the instruments a drum sort of thing made out of the hide of an armadillo?"

"I don't believe it," Vic said, obviously nonplussed. "No one I've ever met knows anything about Andean music. Alice, I think I love you." Alice gasped. "Don't take that seriously," Vic said quickly. "I was just kidding."

"No problem," Alice said, her heartbeat returning to normal. "I know almost nothing about you. What do you do for a living?"

"I create computer games. I'm working on one now, but eventually I'd like to write an X-rated one. I haven't worked out any of the details yet, but it will probably have a super-studly hero who has to kill the bad guys who have taken over a whorehouse. Along the way he stumbles into several rooms and takes part in the fun and games or something like that."

"You're kidding."

"Actually, I'm not. If I ever get the time, I'd love to use a few of your stories as the basis for some of the adventures."

"My stories?" Alice blushed.

"You're a very talented storyteller and the fantasies we've shared live on in my mind."

To change the subject, Alice said, "You talked about an ex-wife so I gather you're divorced. Any kids?"

"I have two teenaged daughters who live with my ex. We've been divorced for almost six years. They live on Long Island and I see them every other weekend, although it's getting harder and harder."

"How come?"

"The girls are growing up and they have their own lives. Both are in high school, and dating and hate to have their social lives messed up with a father." When Alice looked saddened, Vic added quickly, "It's okay, really. They're almost grown and will be in college soon. It's just Dad who has a bit of trouble letting go. It's great that we are really close and talk on the phone often." He paused. "Although they talk to everyone on the phone often."

"Where would any of us be without the phone?" Alice said, grinning.

"Right. How about you? I know you're not married now. Let's forget about that story you told me last week. I assume that was just fiction. Have you ever been married for real?"

Alice told Vic an abbreviated story about Ralph. "He was a nice man whom I never should have married. We got together for all the wrong reasons."

"At least there were no kids to get caught in the middle."

"Amen to that," Alice said.

When the waiter arrived to take dessert orders, Alice hesitated. "Maybe I'll just have coffee."

"Come on, Alice, be brave. Have something completely frivolous. You're entitled for putting up with me all evening."

"I didn't put up with you. I'm having a delightful evening. You're right about dessert, however. I'll have the cheesecake."

Vic grinned. "Make that two."

Alice considered. "Make that one cheesecake with two forks, if that's okay with you, Vic."

"Nice compromise. And two coffees."

As the waiter disappeared, Vic asked, "How did you get connected with Velvet Whispers? Where did you work before that?"

"I work as a receptionist in a dentist's office. You know how long I've been with Velvet Whispers. You were my first call." She told Vic a short version of her connection with Betsy and the discussion that convinced Alice to give it a try.

"You're kidding," Vic said. "I knew I was your first caller at Whispers but I assumed that you had been working somewhere else before. You were so professional and so good at it."

"Thanks for the compliment." Alice beamed.

"You mentioned your mother earlier. Is she better now?"

"No, and she won't be. She's well into her seventies and in really frail health. She's happy, however, at the Rutlandt Nursing Home and my jobs make ends meet." And more, Alice thought. She was actually putting some money in the bank.

"Fortunately my parents are still going strong," Vic said. "My dad works for American Airlines. He was a pilot and my mom was a stewardess when they met."

"How great! Does that mean you get to fly free? I've always wanted to travel."

"I can fly standby, but I seldom do. I used to when my wife and I were still together. We took the kids to Europe every summer, but now it just doesn't happen anymore. I guess I'm too caught up in my work."

"That's really too bad. I always dreamed of going to Europe."

"So come with me. We can tour for a few weeks, see London, Rome, Paris."

"Sure. We can go next week. Don't I wish I could!"

"Why can't you?"

"For starters, my jobs—both of them."

"You could work it out if you wanted to, but we can let that pass for now. By the way, I think we have a little problem regarding your job."

"Oh?" Alice said.

"Well, I'd feel a little silly calling you up on business now."

Alice blushed. "You're right. I would be mortified talking like I do to someone when I've seen his face."

"You mean you couldn't talk dirty to me over the phone."

Alice's color deepened. "Only on a very personal basis, not for money."

Vic took her hand. "Thanks. That's nice." He kept hold of her hand. "Have you ever met any of the other men you talk to?"

"Nope, and if I had, I don't think I could look them in the imaginary eye while I was talking to them. When I don't know them, they're just voices."

"I feel a bit guilty not calling you anymore. Will that louse up your income? I could call and pay, but we could just talk about anything we like."

"Don't be silly. You can call me if you like, but not for money. I have all the callers I can deal with as it is."

"Will you give me your home number?"

Alice considered. In the business she was in, giving out her home phone number was a large step, but she felt completely at home with Vic. As Velvet had said, he was a thoroughly nice and very lonely man. "Sure." They exchanged home addresses and phone numbers.

The waiter arrived with their cheesecake and the conversation wandered into other areas. When they had finished their desserts and their coffee cups had run dry, the check arrived. Vic reached for it. "I'd prefer if we split that," Alice said.

"I come from the old school. The man pays for his dates."

"You said yourself that this isn't a date. Please. I'd feel better."

"Okay. You're right. It's a not-date. Your wish is my command," Vic said. When they had worked out the details and paid the check, he stood to leave. "This has been a wonderful evening," Vic said, helping pull out her chair. "I don't want to rush you, so would you meet me again next week? Same place?"

"Another not-date?"

"I would like to make it a date this time." He placed his hand against the small of Alice's back and guided her through the maze of tables.

"That would be nice. I'd like that."

As they hit the cool, late spring air, Vic leaned over and kissed Alice softly on the lips. "I've enjoyed the evening tremendously. You're nothing like what I expected, and more wonderful."

"Thanks. I've had a great time myself."

They parted without any awkward moments.

The following day, Alice met Betsy in the Italian restaurant in the mall. "Well?" Betsy said as they settled into a booth. "No, don't tell me anything. Velvet's meeting us and you can tell us both."

At that moment, Velvet walked into the darkened room and spotted them immediately. She quickly made herself comfortable in the booth beside Betsy. "Now tell," Velvet said. "Everything."

"He's very nice," Alice said. She told the two women

about the evening in great detail. "We have another date next Tuesday."

"Fan-flippin'-tastic," Betsy said.

"Great," Velvet said. "I have something to tell you, however. I know more about Mr. Sanderson than you might think."

"Yes?" Alice said, terrified that she had dated a mass murderer or a spy.

"When he first called several years ago he said something that triggered something in my brain," Velvet said. "I let it go, but when you said you were going out with him, I looked him up in *Who's Who*. He said he works on computer games." She mentioned a very popular adventure game.

"I know that one," Betsy said. "My boys have it."

"I remember playing it one evening with Phil. He beat me seven ways from Sunday." Alice made the connection. "You mean he worked on that one?"

"He didn't just work on it," Velvet said, conspiratorially. "He invented it. Or wrote it. Or whatever you do to computer games." She mentioned several more very popular games. "Those too. He sold his company last year and made buckets of money. That's how he can afford your phone calls, among other things."

Alice was taken aback. He was rich. That cast a different light on everything. *Oh, shit,* she thought, *I argued about splitting the check. I told him about my problems needing money to support my mother. I probably sounded like a jerk.*

"You said he seemed like a regular guy," Betsy said. "I'll bet he didn't want you to know about all that money. Women don't like to think that they are being courted for their money and maybe he's the same way. He just wanted to be a nice guy you were dating."

"I know," Alice said, "but we're not in the same league."

"Hey wait a minute," Velvet said. "I didn't tell you all that to intimidate you. He's asked you out and that's that."

"I know, but he's not the man he pretended to be."

"Listen," Betsy said. "You aren't Sherry either, but does that change who you really are?"

"You are who you are," Velvet said, "and that's that. So if you had fun, just enjoy and let the chips fall where they may."

Alice sighed. "I guess you're right. Gee. All that money."

"Listen," Velvet said, bringing Alice back from her reverie, "since we're talking about dating, Wayne's got a business friend in from out of town. Interested in dinner? My place, tomorrow evening?"

Alice raised an eyebrow. "A blind date?"

"I guess you could call it that. He's not rich, and since he's from the west coast he's not geographically desirable either, but he's a really nice guy, single again, sort of hunky and cute."

"Single again?"

"Yeah. He's twice divorced, but you're not marrying him, just having dinner with him at my house."

"I don't think so," Alice said.

"Please? I really like him and he seems like a lost ship right now. Just pay a little attention to him and let him feel like a man again. Think of it as a charitable contribution."

Betsy chimed in. "Once again, what have you got to lose?"

"You two are trying to convert me into a social butterfly."

"Hardly," Velvet said. "We had nothing to do with Vic asking you out and this is just a one-night stand." She giggled. "So to speak."

"Come on, Alice. Make the big plunge."

Alice sighed. "Okay you two. How can I argue with both of you?"

"The kids are staying with Wayne's folks overnight so

we'll be able to have a grown-up evening for a change. Wayne's dad will drop them at school Friday morning so I can sleep in and Karen's routing for me so I'm off duty. This is such a pleasure. Can you be at my house about six?"

"As long as the doctor's schedule accommodates. One question. Does he know about your business, about what I do?"

"No. I don't tell too many people, especially Wayne's business associates."

Instead of the jitters she had had before her date with Vic, Thursday passed quickly and easily. Alice had already decided to wear the same gray linen slacks with a white blouse with a thin gray stripe so she dashed home from work and changed quickly. It was a warm late spring evening so instead of a coat, she put on a deep green blazer. After feeding Roger, she made the short drive to Putnam Valley in record time and arrived in Velvet's driveway with two minutes to spare.

"I didn't expect you so promptly," Velvet said as she ushered Alice into the living room. She had met Velvet's husband, Wayne, briefly before and took his outstretched hand warmly. A very ordinary-looking man, he doted on his wife and family and Velvet seemed completely in love with him.

"It's good to see you again," Alice told Wayne and shifted her gaze to the other man in the room. To say he was hunky was an understatement. He looked to be in his mid-thirties, gorgeous in a Kevin Sorbo kind of way. Soft, sandy hair that he wore curling at his shoulders, straight nose, and piercing blue eyes. The tan sports jacket and brown slacks he wore only served to accent his deliciously wide shoulders and narrow hips. Alice found herself wondering what he would look like in Sorbo's Hercules outfit: leather pants and a cloth vest revealing most of his upper body.

"You're Alice," the man said, his voice sounding like hot

fudge. "It's nice to meet you. I'm Todd." He extended his hand and Alice took it. His grip was strong and he held her hand for just a fraction longer than she had expected.

Over drinks before dinner, she learned that Todd was a salesman for a California–based manufacturing firm that did business with Wayne's electronics company. "My business is really deadly dull. Tell me about you."

Alice explained about her job in Dr. Tannenbaum's office. "Do you enjoy what you do?" Todd asked.

"It's a job, and I really like the people I deal with."

"I'm sure they like you too. I know I do."

He really comes on like gangbusters. Slow down, she said, hoping he'd read her. "Thanks. Tell me more about you."

He told her briefly that he was recently out of a messy divorce. "We'd only been married for two years, but it's amazing what you can accumulate in such a short time."

"I'll bet," Alice said.

"You know what we fought about most? Cleopatra." When Alice looked puzzled, he said, "Our brown tabby Persian cat. We each wanted to keep her and it became like a custody battle. Fortunately, about a month into the arguing, we discovered that Cleo was going to have kittens, so my wife got the cat and I got two kittens."

"How wonderful," Alice said. "I don't know how I'd manage without Roger. He's a domestic short hair and my best friend."

"I know what you mean. Cocoa and Cognac are mine."

"Great names."

"Cocoa is a little girl and Cognac is a male. They're all tan and brown so the names seemed to fit."

"What do you do with them when you travel?"

"I have a neighbor who takes care of them for me. You know, cleans the litter pan and puts down new food. They are totally indoor cats so they don't require much."

Somehow, with cats in common, Alice and Todd began to

relax with each other. Over dinner, the group talked about anything and everything, the conversation never lagging, each fighting for an opening to express another opinion. After coffee, they adjourned to the living room with glasses of brandy, where the lively conversation continued until Alice glanced at her watch. "Holy cow," she said. "It's after eleven. I'm going to be useless at work unless I get some sleep." Between her date with Vic, her work Wednesday evening, and the dinner tonight she was going to have to sleep all weekend to make up for it. And she hadn't visited her mother since the previous weekend. She stood, retrieved her jacket, and thanked Velvet and Wayne.

"And Todd, this has been a wonderful evening. I really enjoyed your company."

"I'm going to take off, too, back to my motel. Let me walk you out to your car." He grabbed his jacket, which he had taken off earlier, and slipped it on.

Alice hugged Velvet and planted a quick kiss on Wayne's cheek. "Thanks for dinner. Velvet, I'll talk to you over the weekend."

"Good night," the couple said.

Todd walked Alice to her car. "I'm going to take a risk here," Todd said, and he wrapped his arms around her lightly and leaned forward. Their lips met softly and the tender kiss totally overwhelmed Alice's senses. She pulled back slightly and looked at Todd in the moonlight. It had been years since she'd been kissed and she discovered that she liked it. She leaned forward again, touched her lips to his and sighed.

Todd made a soft sound deep in his throat and gently pressed her back against her car door. The feeling of being trapped against the cool metal made Alice tremble. Todd jumped back. "I'm sorry. I got carried away."

Alice cupped his face in her hands. "Don't be sorry. It was really nice."

Todd grinned. Then he tangled his fingers in her short curls and brought her face to his. Again they kissed, this one no longer tender. Now his mouth was hungry, heating her body and moistening her. When he pulled back, he gazed into her eyes. "My God, woman. No one should be allowed to kiss like that."

Alice was puzzled. "Like what?"

"Like you're a great vortex and I'm yearning to fall in. I want to devour you and your mouth tells me that you want it too."

Was that what her mouth was saying? It had been so long. Maybe the combination of her long time away from men and her conversations over the phone had changed her from the woman Ralph divorced to something more. Todd kissed her again, and this time she melted into it, letting her tongue roam at will, testing things she had talked about but never done. She slid her hands up his back beneath his jacket, questing the warmth of his body through his shirt. He pressed his obvious erection against her lower body and she allowed her body to press back.

They broke the kiss and, panting, she let her head fall back as Todd kissed his way down her throat. His hands slid up the sides of her shirt until his palms held her ribs and his thumbs brushed the tips of her breasts. She felt her nipples harden and her thighs shake. Without the support of her car against her back, she would have fallen from the sheer eroticism of it all.

"What's going on here?" Todd asked, his voice breathy and hoarse. "This is crazy."

Obviously he felt the burst of passion too. "I know. I have to tell you that I haven't kissed anyone in a very long time."

"I'd like to do a lot more than kiss you. I'm aching for you and this isn't the way I would have this happen."

"Why?" she whispered.

"My home's three thousand miles away and I don't get

here more than once or twice a year. I'm leaving on Tuesday to other places, other people."

"Other women?"

"Yes, and I want to make that clear up front. I have other female friends and I don't deny it. But I've never had anything hit me so hard and so suddenly and after such a short time. I want to bury myself in you until we're too exhausted to move. I want to feel you beneath me. I want to make you scream and beg and cry for it, then make you climax over and over."

Alice hadn't said it any better to any of her clients. Was it a line? Maybe. He certainly knew what buttons to push and how to push them. But was that bad? Didn't she feel the same things? "So what should we do about it?"

"Ordinarily I'd ask you out a few more times, then try to convince you to join me in bed. We don't have a few more times. Can I see you tomorrow night?"

It was Friday and she had a regular caller. "I'm afraid I have something else I have to do."

He sighed and backed away. "I understand."

She shouldn't do this. Not for any reason. Except one. She wanted to. "No, you don't. I can't tomorrow, but I'm free Saturday." She didn't confuse love and lust. This was sexual, pure and simple, and from all of her phone relationships she had learned that there was nothing wrong with sexuality just for fun. And this was going to be fun, pure and hopefully simple.

In the dim light, she could see his eyes light up. "That's great. I'll call you during the day on Saturday and we'll make plans. Pick someplace nice and we can talk. Get to know each other better. That's the place to start."

Alice didn't have to ask what they were starting. It was obvious. Something really short term and really explosive.

"Yes, it is." They exchanged phone numbers and Alice got into her car. Before she closed the door, Todd kissed her again. The kiss was just as incendiary as the last, leaving Alice's hands shaking and her mind numb. Nothing even vaguely resembling this had ever happened to her before or would probably happen to her again. She didn't care.

"Until Saturday," she said.

"Until Saturday."

Chapter 10

"So tell me about Todd," Betsy said to Alice the following morning.

"He's sexy as hell and we have a date Saturday night."

"Wonderful. Tell me everything."

"Listen. I know that this is a short-time thing. No hearts and flowers, no," she made quoting marks in the air, "*relationship*, and I really want to keep it to myself for a little while."

"Are you okay?" Betsy asked, obviously a bit put out at Alice for not sharing.

"I'm great." She gave her friend a quick hug. "I just want this to be all my decision. If I talk about it, I might change my mind and I don't want to. For once in my life I don't want to be logical."

"Hey, I wouldn't ask you to change anything. Does what you're doing feel right?"

"I'm not sure, but it feels like another 'What have I got to lose' so I'm going to wing it."

Betsy hugged her friend back. "Good for you. Have a blast."

She was going to do just that. She was going to invite Todd to her apartment for dinner and let things happen whatever way they happened. She wanted it and it was about time she took something just because she wanted it. She talked to her sister Friday evening and made plans to visit her mother on Sunday. Then, after work on Saturday, she dashed to the market and bought a thick sirloin steak, a rice mix that cooked in fifteen minutes, salad makings, and a package of frozen vegetables. Then she stopped at the liquor store and picked up a bottle of nice red wine and a bottle of rather expensive brandy, the drink that Todd had had after dinner on Thursday. Then she decided on one more stop, at a local convenience store for a three-pack of condoms. If what she expected to happen happened, she would be ready.

At home she quickly made a salad and put it into the refrigerator. It was not yet five so Alice decided that she had enough time for a bath. She turned on the hot water in the tub and poured a capful of bubble liquid beneath the tap. As the bath ran, she stripped off her clothes and stared into her closet. She quickly decided on a soft cotton sweater in a becoming shade of light blue, her softest jeans, and a pair of loafers. Easy on, easy off, she thought. Then she stashed the condoms in the table beside the bed and looked around the bedroom.

The previous evening, between phone calls she had tidied up and this morning she had changed the sheets. Three weeks before she had bought new drapes and a matching quilt in a pink and green floral pattern, and had coordinated several pillows. *Well,* she thought, *that's the best I can do.*

Back in the bathroom, she turned off the water and

climbed into the tub. With a chirrup, Roger jumped onto the toilet seat. Tail swishing, he reached out a paw and batted at the mound of bubbles just within his reach. "I know," Alice said. "You're not used to this, are you."

Merrow.

"Well, I'm not either, but I'm not too old to learn, so I'm going to do just that. It's a hell of about time, don't you think?"

Roger batted at the bubbles, his paw now covered with foam. When he started to lick it off, he sneezed. "See? Something new for all of us."

Fascinated, Roger spent the next fifteen minutes trying to understand bubbles while Alice relaxed in the tub, surprised that she wasn't more nervous. "You know, Roger," she said, finally standing up and grabbing a bath towel, "I should be really upset about this. If everything goes all right I'm about to get into what several of my callers refer to as sport fucking." She wrinkled her nose and stepped out of the tub. "Ugh. That sounds terrible, but I guess that's what it is. It's not lovemaking since there's no love involved, but it's not going to be just fucking either. It's going to be two people doing things that feel wonderful."

Merrow.

"Right. He's really cute too. Wait till you see. He likes cats but you stay out of the way. Hear?"

In her bedroom, she opened her underwear drawer. She had nothing particularly sexy, nothing like the lingerie she described in such detail three nights a week, so she did the best she could. She pulled out a stretchy, beige nylon bra and matching bikini panties. "I wish I had something lacy," she said to Roger, now washing his front paws in the middle of her new quilt. "I'll have to take some time next week and shop, in case this happens again."

Roger rolled over and Alice sat on the bed and scratched his belly. Roger's purr filled the room as Alice dressed. At ten minutes to six, Alice faced herself in the mirror. She smoothed on eyeliner, redoing it twice before it looked the way she wanted it to, then added soft pink blush and lipstick. She considered mascara, but rejected the idea. Who knew when it might smear, and under what conditions? She fluffed her short curls, unable to do anything to her hair that it didn't want. She added small pearl earrings and a strand of pearls that rested between her breasts.

She started out of the bathroom, then quickly took a small bottle of Opium that Betsy had given her last Christmas, and dabbed just a touch behind each ear and in her cleavage. "Ready as ever," she said to Roger, now fast asleep on the bed. "You'd better stay out from underfoot."

As she closed the bedroom door behind her, the doorbell rang. Her heart lurched but she calmly walked to the front door. Todd stood in front of her apartment dressed in a navy-blue blazer, gray slacks, and a yellow knit shirt. His eyes were even bluer than she remembered and gazed at her in appreciation, and puzzlement. "Hi. Am I overdressed for wherever we're going?"

"Not at all," Alice said ushering him inside. "Actually I thought we could eat here. I'm not a great cook but I broil a mean steak."

Todd grinned. "Great idea. Come here." He reached for her and drew her into his arms. "I've been thinking about this for two very long days." His lips met hers and the electricity she had felt when they first kissed surged through her again. His hands alternately massaged her back and grabbed her hair. "You know," he said when they paused to catch their breath, "I've been thinking about you and about this evening." He released her and walked into the living room. "I don't want to pressure you or anything. We're both grown-ups. I want you. I want to make love to you, with you. I don't want you to think I jump on every woman I meet but this isn't true love either. I don't want any confusion."

When she didn't respond, he continued, "I don't want anything going on under false pretenses."

Alice walked up to him and smiled. "I understand everything and I don't jump every man I meet either. Can I take your jacket?"

His grin made him look about ten years younger. He slipped his jacket off his shoulders and dropped it on the sofa. "Come here." He tangled his fingers in her hair and gently pulled her head back, then buried his mouth in the hollow at the base of her throat.

This is exactly what I wanted, Alice thought in the small part of her mind that could still think. Then that section shut down beneath the onslaught of her senses. His mouth was hot, his tongue rough as he licked the tender spot where her shoulder met her neck. His hands roamed up her sides until his thumbs brushed the lower curves of her breasts. She thought about foreplay and the slow building from embers to flames, but the flames already existed and were quickly devouring both of them.

She combed her fingers through his hair, marveling at the softness. Like baby hair, she thought. His hands were beneath her sweater now, branding her bare skin everywhere he touched. One hand cupped her buttocks and pressed her lower body against the hard ridge of flesh beneath the crotch of his slacks. "God," he purred, "I can't get close enough to you."

She marveled at the core of calm and rational enjoyment that existed beneath the raging fires that consumed her conscious mind. This was what she had been talking about all these weeks. She took the lower edge of her sweater in her hands and pulled it over her head. Then she grabbed his shirt and did the same. "Better," she whispered, rubbing her hands over his chest, sliding her fingers through the light furring of blond hair.

"This too," he growled, unhooking her bra and dragging

it off. "God yes." He cupped her breasts, his thumbs flicking over her already erect nipples. "Yes. So good."

Alice's knees threatened to buckle. "In here," she said, the words difficult to get past the passion in her throat. She led him to the bedroom and, as she opened the door, Roger trotted through. He stopped to sniff Todd's slacks, then rubbed briefly against his legs and headed off toward the kitchen.

"I'm not usually this impatient," Todd said as he entered Alice's bedroom, his fingers working at the fastenings of her jeans, "but I don't seem to be rushing you."

"You're not," Alice said, smiling at his assumption that she was an old hand at all of this. She pushed the door closed.

Quickly they removed their remaining clothes and, both naked, fell onto the bed. Todd's mouth found Alice's nipple and her back arched as shards of electric pleasure knifed through her. His fingers pinched the other nipple, causing pain that was both sharp and erotic.

She had talked about women's hands on men's cocks for weeks but she had never actually held a man's penis in her hands before. Now she touched him and he felt wonderful, like velvet over rigid muscle. His skin was soft and hot as she held him, squeezing gently.

"Do that any more and I'll lose it right here," he said hoarsely, moving her hand away.

Then his fingers slipped between her legs and found her hot and wet. "Yes," she whispered. "Oh yes." He touched and explored, then slid one finger into her channel. "Oh shit," she hissed, her back arching and her hips driving his hands against her.

When he withdrew she felt bereft, but then she heard the ripping of paper and understood. Only moments later his condom-covered cock pressed at her entrance and with one thrust Todd buried himself inside of her. It was fast, hot, and hard, Todd's hips pounding and Alice's legs wrapped around his waist. They clawed at each other's backs trying to drive deeper.

"Touch me," she cried and Todd's fingers slipped between them and found her clit. With a shout he came, and then, only moments later, Alice felt the familiar bubble growing low in her belly. Todd was still driving into her, his body spasming when she exploded, her orgasm bigger than any she had created for herself.

"God, baby," Todd said later as they calmed. "You're something."

"You're not bad yourself," Alice said. "That was amazing."

"You're amazing," he said, using a tissue to clean himself up. Then he rolled over and cuddled her against his side, her head on his shoulder. "I love a woman who enjoys good sex. There's nothing coy or reticent about you. It's wonderful."

Alice thought about what had happened. She had enjoyed it. More than that, it had been one of the greatest experiences of her life. Nothing that she had had with Ralph had prepared her for the unbridled passion of what she and Todd had done. It seemed so simple.

They had dinner and, over coffee and brandy, Todd kissed her again, more slowly this time as hands and mouths discovered erotic places. For the first time Alice touched a man's cock and was delighted when she obviously excited him. She knew what she had read and talked about, and whatever she did seemed to please Todd. When Todd touched his tongue to her clit, Alice thought she would fly into space and, with his mouth lightly sucking on her flesh and his fingers inside her pussy, she came. "God, woman, you're so responsive." Then he was inside of her and she came again as he did. They pulled the quilt over them later and, with Roger on the bed beside them, they slept until the following morning.

Todd was still asleep when Alice awoke the next day. She lay quietly and thought about the previous night. It had been wonderful, fulfilling, and electric. She had no regrets about anything and that surprised her. For weeks she had been talking a good game, and now she was playing. It was sensational. She stretched, slipped from the bed, and padded to the bathroom.

Minutes later she stood in the shower under the warm spray. She lathered her body and wondered at the slick, slipperiness of her skin. She felt her hands on her flesh and tried to feel what Todd had felt. She wasn't pretty, she didn't have a sexy body, but he had seemed to really like touching her and making love to her. In her stories she was always the ideal-looking person she had always dreamed about, but now it didn't seem to matter. Todd was gorgeous and that was what had attracted her in the first place, but after the first few minutes, it was his love of cats and his sense of humor that had kept her interest.

Suddenly the shower curtain moved and Todd climbed into the tub behind her. "Good morning."

She thought she'd feel awkward after all that they had done the previous evening, but she didn't. "Good morning. I have to visit my mom today so I thought I'd get started early so maybe we could get together again later."

"A woman with a plan. I like that. But must we waste this wonderful opportunity?" He took the shower scrubby that she used with her body wash, squeezed a large amount of aromatic gel onto it, and began to lather her body. Slowly he soaped her skin, taking time to cover her breasts and mound with bubbles. She parted her legs as he slipped the plastic sponge between her thighs and caressed her pussy with it. As he rinsed her off, she took the sponge from him and moved him beneath the spray so his back was turned toward her.

With more lather on the pink sponge, she slowly stroked

it over his back, taking time to appreciate his tight buttocks. She remembered a story she had told several times about a couple who made love in a shower and she realized that she had a perfect opportunity to get to know Todd's body better. She crouched and washed down the backs of his thighs and felt him tremble as she parted his cheeks and rubbed that hidden valley between.

Water cascaded over her head as she turned him and washed his feet and the fronts of his legs. Then she stood and lathered his softly furred chest and shoulders, his arms and hands. Now she could move to the part of his body she was most interested in. She put more gel on the sponge and knelt, stroking the slightly rough surface over his semierect penis. She allowed herself to look at his body and watch his penis react to her ministrations. She lifted his cock and gently scrubbed his testicles, then rubbed the tender area behind. As she touched, she watched his cock react and twitch, making his enjoyment obvious. She slid her fingers between his thighs and touched the slippery skin behind his balls, then slipped further backward and touched his anus. His knees almost gave out.

She had touched his erection the previous evening but now she wondered whether she could take it into her mouth as the women had in her stories. Still touching his balls and asshole, she licked the falling water from the tip of his cock with the flat of her tongue. Todd grabbed her shoulders. "Don't do that, baby," he groaned. "If you do, I'll shoot right here and now."

"Is there a problem with that?"

"Oh, God."

She was going to do it. She didn't think she could deep-throat it as her characters often did in her stories, but she drew the end of Todd's cock into her mouth. She created a vacuum and pulled her head back, creating suction. Todd tangled his fingers in her hair and held her tightly, more for his own balance than to restrain her. She felt his muscles tighten and knew that he was ready to climax. "Baby," he shouted. She wrapped one hand around his erection, feeling it swell and jerk.

She wanted to taste his come, but she didn't think she could swallow it so she opened her mouth and, as jets of thick, white jism shot from Todd's cock, she allowed most of it to flow from between her lips. The fluid was thick and viscous and tasted slightly tangy. She avidly watched his cock and her hand and she instinctively pumped the last of his climax.

"Shit, baby," Todd said. "That's not fair."

"What's not fair?" Alice said, a grin splitting her face.

"You did that to me and I didn't satisfy you."

"I am satisfied. That was amazing."

Together they lathered and rinsed and, wrapped in thick towels, wandered back into the bedroom. As Alice rubbed her curls dry, she felt herself grabbed from behind. "Get over here," Todd said. He pulled her toward the bed and then pushed her down. "We're going to play a little game," he growled. "You're going to lie there and I'm going to do to you what you just did to me."

Alice giggled and tried to get up. "That's not necessary. This isn't a tit-for-tat kind of thing. I enjoyed what happened and that's that."

"Tit for tat, eh? Well I want those tits, do you understand? Now lie down," he snapped and pushed her back onto the bed.

Alice suddenly stopped laughing. "Yes, sir," she said softly. She settled back onto the bed. There was suddenly nothing soft about Todd. There was a hard edge to his voice, ordering her to follow his instructions. She felt herself tremble with excitement.

"That's more like it. Now, spread your legs and make it quick." He stood at the foot of the bed, arms crossed over his naked chest. He was beautiful, powerful.

She did as he commanded and felt herself immediately wet. "Wider," he snapped.

Alice spread her legs as wide as they would go while Todd looked down at her. "You like that, don't you?" he said, his question not requiring an answer. "I suspected that you would. I love giving orders and seeing a beautiful woman obey."

Obey. The word made her body jolt. She did like it. Very much.

Todd parted her towel and stared at her. "I want to suck your tits. Offer one to me."

What was it that made her cup her flattened breast and hold it for him? The mastery? His aura of command? The domination? It was all of those and more, she realized.

He knelt beside the bed and placed his mouth on her fully erect nipple. She felt his teeth bite down, just enough to cause her pain. When she grunted, he said, "I wanted to do that and you wanted me to. You want this and both of us know it. Is this new for you?"

"Yes," she whispered. It was all new to her and now she wanted it all.

He grabbed her hair and held her head against the mattress. Then he ravished her mouth. There was no gentleness, but rather power and hunger. When he leaned back, he said, "Since I climaxed before, I'm not feeling impatient to have you. You're mine and I can do whatever I like to you. And I'm in no hurry." He settled onto the edge of the bed. "I've played a lot of games with women," he said as Alice stared at him. "I love sex in all forms. Now it seems I've discovered something that makes you crazy." He rubbed his finger through her sopping pussy. "Oh yes," he said. "So wet. This obviously makes you hungry."

He pulled off his towel and stretched out on top of her, his feet holding hers down and his hands grasping her wrists. She could feel the length of his body against hers and her heart pounded. His mouth devoured hers while he held her so she couldn't move. Briefly Alice wondered whether she should be reacting this way, then she stopped caring. Over the weeks she had been telling stories, she realized that everyone had their pleasures and she was entitled to feel whatever she felt and enjoy whatever gave her pleasure. And this did.

Todd stood up. "You are not to move. Just lie there with your legs wide apart and let me do whatever I want."

She choked out the word, "Yes."

Todd spent long minutes playing with her breasts. He kissed, licked, sucked, and bit until it was all Alice could do not to grab him and make him satisfy the gnawing hunger he was creating. Yet she didn't move. It had become a challenge. He had told her not to move and she wouldn't.

Finally he moved between her spread legs and gazed at her pussy. "I'll bet you've never seen a pussy," he said, "but they are so beautiful. Yours is so wet I can see the moisture." He touched her inner lips with one finger. "God, you're so hot, baby." He touched the end of her clit lightly and her hips jumped. "I told you not to move," he growled.

She concentrated on keeping her body still. "That's better," he said. He looked around the bedroom and she could see him stare at the candle she had in a holder on her dresser. She had intended to light it the previous evening but things had proceeded so quickly that she had not had the chance. He stood up and grabbed the candle, a taper about eight inches long and over an inch in diameter. He hurried into the bathroom and Alice could hear the water running. Knowing what he must have in mind, Alice felt her muscles tighten.

He returned with the candle in his hand. "See this? You've figured out what I'm going to do with it, haven't you."

She nodded.

He settled back between her legs and rubbed the wax

through the folds of her pussy then over her clit. "Here's what I'm going to do. I'm going to fuck you with this dildo. I'm going to slowly force it into your beautiful pussy. It might be a bit bigger than a cock but your body will take it, and you won't move while I do it. Then I'm going to suck your clit and I'm going to feel you come. Being fucked with a candle and having me in control of your body will make you so hot that you won't be able to help it. You won't be in control of it, I will."

He placed the candle against the opening of her pussy and, ever so slowly, pushed it into her body. It was larger than any cock she had felt and it seemed to force its way into her. Alice had never had anything but fingers and cocks inside of her and she noticed with the rational part of her brain that the candle felt cool and filled her in a way that no cock had. Deeper and deeper it penetrated until it seemed to fill not only her body but her mind. She was overwhelmed with sensations and Todd now pulled, now pushed, fucking her with the candle.

She was so close, she realized. So close that when his mouth found her clit she came, screaming. Her hips bucked so hard it was difficult for him to keep his mouth on her, but he did, pulling on her clit and drawing the climax out longer and longer. She couldn't control her body as wave after wave crashed over her. For long minutes she came and came. She finally placed her hand against his forehead and gently pushed him away.

Totally limp, she lay still as Todd climbed up the bed and settled against her side. He cradled her head against him and kissed her curls. "My god, woman. I've never seen anyone come like that. You're incredible."

"That was incredible," she whispered, unable to make any louder sound. They dozed for another hour, then dressed quickly. "I don't have anything in the house for breakfast," Alice admitted.

"Then how about the diner?" he asked.

"Sure. I've got to be at my mom's nursing home at noon so we've got some time."

"Can we get together again tonight?" Todd asked.

"I was hoping to. I'll be back here about five." She had planned to do some writing for her clients, but that would have to wait. After this morning she had so much to say and there was no possibility that she would forget any of it.

Alice and Todd talked almost nonstop while they ate and Todd kissed her deeply as they parted, to meet at her place at five-thirty. As she drove south she smiled. It had been so fantastic and she had learned a lot about herself.

Her mom seemed to be doing a bit better and Sue arrived at the nursing home at about one. Together the three women sat in the sunny garden and although she said nothing, her mother seemed to be enjoying the conversation. "Are you okay with the money?" Sue asked at one point.

"Yes. My new job is fun and pays well. I can afford this without any problem. Don't worry about a thing."

"Well, I don't think I've ever seen you look better. You've got a glow. Whatever you're doing must agree with you."

If you only knew, Alice thought.

Chapter 11

Todd arrived at Alice's apartment at five-thirty that evening with a pizza in hand. They both knew that going out to dinner wasn't going to happen so they made quick work of the pie and ended up in bed again. They made love twice that evening and again at 3:00 A.M. When the alarm rang at seven, Todd reached for her again. "Sorry," she said, "but I have to be at work at eight and a shower and a bowl of cereal are a necessity."

"Oh, baby," Todd groaned. "You're such a spoilsport."

Alice kissed him thoroughly, then said, "You can stay in bed if you like, but I'm out of here." When she returned from the bathroom, Todd was already dressed.

"I have a nine o'clock meeting that I have to dress for anyway so I thought I'd go back to my motel and shower and change there." He dragged her close. "Tonight?"

"I'm sorry, I can't."

Todd's eyes widened. "I had hoped . . ."

"I wish I could, but I can't. I have a commitment I can't change." She had three regular callers who were in for a surprise that night. She had several stories whirling in her head, all based on what she had experienced all weekend.

"I'm flying out at noon on Tuesday," Todd pouted.

Alice put her arms around him. "I know and I wish there were something I could do, but there isn't. I just can't."

"I'll see whether I can arrange a trip to New York in the fall."

Alice beamed. "Wonderful. I'll look forward to that. In the meantime, we'll e-mail and call each other."

"It won't be the same. We've only known each other for a few days but . . ."

"Don't. You said you've got other female friends and I've got men I date too. Let's just leave it that it's been great and we'll do it again when we can."

"You sound like me. I'm usually the one who makes that speech."

"Well then, you're usually the wise one."

Alice could feel Todd's chuckle deep in his chest. "It feels really strange to be on the receiving end." He pulled away and slapped her lightly on the bottom. "All right, woman, let's get going."

Alice arrived at Dr. Tannenbaum's office at exactly eight o'clock to find Betsy on the phone and the doctor's first patient sitting in the waiting room reading a magazine. Betsy put her hand over the mouthpiece of the receiver. "He's going to be about fifteen minutes late."

"Oh, Mr. Fucito," Alice said to the waiting patient as she hung up her coat. "I'm sorry. I'm sure it was unavoidable."

"No problem, Alice," the man said. "I'm not due at work until ten-thirty."

As she arrived in the reception area, Alice tried unsuccessfully to wipe off the grin that had been on her face all morning. "You look like a cat who's just eaten several very fat canaries," Betsy said. "What gives?"

"I had a weekend to write stories about."

"Tell all, and quickly."

The phone rang and Alice adjusted an appointment for the following morning. As she hung up, she said, "About this weekend . . ."

The door opened and Dr. Tannenbaum arrived with a flurry of questions and instructions. "Listen," Betsy said. "We're never going to get a chance to talk here. I know you usually have errands to run at lunch but I'm meeting Velvet. Come along and you can regale us with your weekend adventures."

Alice couldn't suppress her grin. She wanted to keep it all to herself, but she also wanted to crow a bit. "Done." Betsy disappeared into the operatory and Alice returned to her computer.

At ten after one, the three women were seated in a booth at a diner and had already ordered sandwiches and drinks. "All right," Betsy said. "Enough stalling. Tell us everything."

"You had a date with Todd," Velvet said.

"You might say that." Alice burst out laughing, then filled the two women in on her adventures of the weekend.

"Wow. A one-weekend stand," Velvet said. "God, I envy you."

"Why?" Alice said, genuinely puzzled. "Isn't Wayne good? You know what I mean."

"He's great, but there's no thrill like a new man and the adventure of new and great sex."

"As good as Larry is," Betsy added, "and we're very in tune and totally compatible, first times are something totally different, the stuff fantasies are made of."

"Well this was certainly the stuff of fantasies," Alice said, sipping her soda. "It's like I've discovered a new toy. I knew creative sex existed and I've made up dozens of stories about it, but that was from the outside looking in. Now I've opened Pandora's box and I want to sample everything inside." She thought about the catalog Betsy had given her that she had never gotten around to exploring. "I want it all."

"And you should have it," Betsy said. "Good sex is the best stuff. I know from experience."

"Are you going to see Todd again before he leaves?" Velvet asked.

"Unfortunately, no. He's leaving tomorrow and I have callers tonight."

"That's really sad."

"No, it's really not," Alice said. "This was a slice out of a fantasy. It's not real and in some ways I wouldn't want it to become too real."

"Like how?" Betsy asked.

"I don't want to know what he's like when he's cranky, or sick. I don't know whether we have much in common and this way it doesn't matter. It was neat, and now it's done. Maybe we'll do it again, and maybe not but it's all okay."

"Aren't you sad that it was so short?" Betsy continued. "I mean, that might have become something more permanent. Don't you want that?"

"In some ways I do, but this wasn't it. If he were a local, we would have dated and gotten to know each other before we ended up in bed together and that's the basis of something more. Like Vic and I are doing. Since this weekend I have a bit more of an open mind about men and dating now that I've found out more about the real me."

"Who's the real you?"

"Someone who enjoys sex for the sake of sex."

"Indulging in one-night stands isn't life. It's not real," Betsy said.

"Exactly and I know that, but it's not wrong either.

Obviously if someone comes along and we hit it off, that's wonderful. For the moment, however, I want to experiment, to explore, to experience firsthand all the things I've talked about with my callers. I want to play."

"What about Vic?" Velvet asked.

"We're meeting tomorrow night for dinner."

"Which category does he fit into?" Betsy asked.

"I haven't the faintest idea." She raised her glass. "Here's to not knowing and not caring." The three women touched glasses and toasted.

That evening Sheherazade's stories took on a new dimension. They were a bit more adventurous and there was a special music in her voice. Two of her regular callers noticed and told her that they enjoyed her tales even more than usual.

The following evening, Alice met Vic for dinner. The evening passed delightfully quickly, with good conversation and lots of laughter. There were moments when Alice thought about her split personality. Although she and Vic had become acquainted through their phone calls, so far their two "dates" had been chaste with no conversation about sex in any form.

As they sipped coffee, Vic asked, "Can I see you next Saturday? Like a real Saturday night date?"

"I'd like that." Alice stared at Vic's hands that now surrounded his coffee cup. Short, blunt fingers, wide palms. Nice, functional hands. How would they feel touching her? she wondered. *Stop that,* she told herself. *Every man isn't Todd. Every evening isn't a prelude to a romp in bed.*

"I'd love to find someplace a bit more subdued. All this green and white has me wondering whether I'm growing roots."

Alice's smile widened. "I'm not too familiar with this area. How far north do you want to drive?"

Vic winked. "Your place?" Over the sound of her breath

catching in her throat, Vic continued, "I'm so sorry. I promised myself that I wouldn't mention anything like that. I don't want you to think that I'm here because of the way we met. I mean I'm not after sex. I mean . . ." Obviously frustrated, Vic ran his fingers through his shaggy hair.

"Whoa," Alice said. "Sex doesn't have to be a taboo topic between us. We met under really bizarre circumstances so maybe it's a bit awkward but we can't trip over our tongues either."

"I know, but I don't want you to get the wrong idea."

"I won't. When two people get to know each other, like we are, it's natural that the conversation will eventually turn to sexual topics. We both understand that I'm not Sheherazade. I'm just plain Alice Waterman but I'm not a prude either." *Certainly not a prude anymore,* she thought.

"You're a delightfully creative person and I think you're terrific." Alice could see Vic begin to blush. It was strange how different he was in person from the sexy man she had known over the phone. "Let's change the subject. Is next Saturday evening okay with you?"

"I'd like that. There's a great little place in Brewster that has good food and a small dance floor. Do you like to dance?"

"I love it," Vic said.

She'd been to a few dances in high school but had gotten discouraged when the only boys who asked her to dance had had octopus hands and were interested in where they could touch. She liked music and had tried to talk Ralph into going out a few times, to no avail.

"Great. Let me check on the name of the place and I'll get directions for you and call you later in the week."

As they approached her car in the parking lot, Vic became silent. "Alice, this is really bothering me."

"What is?"

"I want to kiss you good night but I'm in that same bind

I was in before. I don't want you to get the wrong idea."

Alice turned and cupped Vic's face with her palms. "This is really silly." She touched his lips, softly tasting his mouth. As they kissed, she felt his hands lightly stroke her back. She couldn't help contrast this kiss with the toe-curling ones she had shared with Todd. This was entirely different, soft, shy, questioning, hopeful.

"Phew," Vic said as they separated. "Maybe there's more of Sheherazade in you than you know." He kissed her this time and she enjoyed the undemanding feel of his mouth on hers.

"Nice," she purred. "Very nice." Unwilling to go any further yet, she turned and unlocked her car. "I'll call you."

As she settled behind the wheel, Vic leaned over and kissed her again. "I'll look forward to that."

Nice man, she thought as she started her car. Nice, uncomplicated man.

When she got home, she found that she wasn't tired. Betsy's catalog lay on her dresser waiting for her to have some time to look through it, so she picked it up and stretched out on the bed. With his usual chirrup, Roger leaped up beside her and stretched out on his back. Idly scratching the cat's stomach, Alice propped the catalog on her raised knees and looked at the model on the front cover. "I guess that's what my guys think Sheherazade looks like," she said. "What do you think, Roger? Nothing that ten years, a face-lift, twenty-five pounds, and the right makeup wouldn't fix. Right?"

Merrow.

She flipped to an inside page. "Oh my," she said, gazing at a page full of dildos, in all colors, shapes, and textures. "I never imagined that anyone would want one of those in hot pink." Actually, she'd never imagined anyone owning one until she began telling her stories. She turned the page and found vibrators in almost as many varieties. As she thumbed through the thick catalog, she found lubes, anal plugs, cock rings, and several devices she didn't quite understand. She also found that her body responded to the pictures and the ideas they fostered. "I guess it's all research," she told the cat.

For a second time, she went through the catalog and decided to order several items. She noticed that the company had a Web site so, thinking it would be easier and less personal to purchase that way, she logged on and placed an order for a three-dildo collection and a battery-operated vibrator. Now anxious to receive the objects, she clicked on the overnight delivery icon, gave her credit-card number, and logged off. "Well, Roger, I've now ordered my first sex toys. Am I a sophisticate or what?"

Friday, when she arrived home from work, the package was waiting on her doorstep. She had almost two hours before her first client, so she made herself a peanut-butter and jelly sandwich and poured herself a diet soda. Dinner and package in hand, she adjourned to the bedroom. Still chewing her first bite, she grabbed a pair of scissors and stabbed at the tape. Finally the box opened. "Well, Pandora, I know just how you must have felt."

On top of the packaging material she found lots of literature from the company with this month's specials, movies for sale, and three paper folders from affiliated companies. As she placed them on the bed beside her, she noticed that one was for an erotic book sales business, one from a company that specialized in leather items, and one from a phone-sex line. She looked more carefully at the slick paper phone-sex ad. HOT WOMEN WITH SOPPING PUSSIES ANXIOUS FOR YOUR PRICK, one headline read. "Makes what I do sound so dirty," she said. "Amazing."

Beneath the literature, she found two boxes, one with her dildos and one with the vibrator. She opened the dildo box first. Each of the objects inside resembled an erect penis, one in soft pink plastic, about one inch in diameter with thick ridges at half-inch intervals down the shaft; one blue, shorter than the first and very thick around; and a third in soft green plastic curved to, as the box indicated, "stimulate her G-spot." She placed the three on their wide bases on the bed-table and giggled. "Three blind mice," she sang. "Oh Roger, this is so silly." Roger sniffed at the now-empty box, then put his front paws on the bedside table and sniffed at the three dildos. Then he sneezed from the plastic smell and settled on the bed. "Right attitude," Alice said.

She opened the box with the vibrator and looked at each of the tips that came with it. One was flat, with little cup-like structures all over it, one a soft nob, one a long slender rod that was for insertion and one with a long shaft with a ball at the end covered with soft, inchlong flexible fingers of latex. "Looks like the Spanish inquisition to me, but I won't dismiss any of it. Some women must like it."

She munched on her sandwich and let her mind wander. Toys. They hadn't played much of a part in her stories up to now, but with this inspiration, she might just create something new for one of her callers tonight. She also understood that as strange as these items might appear when she was calm and cool, when she was aroused, they would look entirely different. She thought about the lipstick she had used many times as a dildo. Now she had the real thing and ideas flooded her mind.

Her first caller was new and she used a story she'd told several times in the past. When she was done, she was pleased, especially when he asked whether he could call again. Her second was a regular and she continued the story she had begun several weeks earlier.

Her third caller was a man named Jacques whom Alice

had spoken to a few times. Many men used assumed names and tried to change the tone of their voice when they called her so it didn't faze her that Jacques put on a thick French accent when they spoke. He also had a delightfully creative mind. Once he had even helped with a story, making suggestions about what the characters should do. Alice gazed at the three dildos still lined up on the table beside her bed. Jacques was the perfect man for a story that had been smouldering in her mind all night.

"Jacques, you sweet thing," she said when the router put him through. "I've been waiting for you."

"I've been waiting for you too, *cherie,*" Jacques said. His accent was particularly thick that evening. She had no idea what he looked like, but even though the accent was phony, he sounded sexy as hell.

"I thought I'd tell you about a date I had a few years ago."

"Ohh," Jacques said. "I wish you would date me."

"Well, if you keep sounding so sexy, I just might."

"If I'm ever where you are, maybe we can be together."

"Well, you keep asking and maybe I'll break down one of these days." She knew this was all talk since neither of them had any idea where the other was. "What if I call the man Jacques? Then we can pretend that we were there together."

"Marvelous," he said. "I don't want to think of you with other men. Me, I would please you so much you wouldn't need anyone else."

"Oh, I know you would. Anyway," Alice began, "it was summer. Jacques and I had dated about a dozen times and, since we stayed up late making love one Saturday night, we had decided that he would stay over. Now it was morning and, when I woke up I found that his side of the bed was empty. Puzzled I got up and headed for the bathroom. On the counter beside the sink I found a large box with a note that said,

DO NOT OPEN UNTIL EXACTLY 9:00 A.M. THEN UNWRAP
THIS AND FOLLOW THE INSTRUCTIONS INSIDE TO THE LET-
TER! I'LL PICK YOU UP AT 10:00.

"It was only seven-thirty but I couldn't wait to see what
was inside the large box. As I started to untie the bright
red ribbon my eyes found the note again. . . exactly 9:00
A.M. . . . *What the hell,* I thought, *I'll play along.* Thinking
about what might be in the box was making my nerve
endings tingle."

"That sounds like quite a date you had. Tell me about the
man. Was he tall like me, with big biceps and big shoulders?
I'm big all over, you know."

"I'll bet you are," Alice said, grinning. "Actually he was-
n't much to look at, but he had a gleam in his eye and a very
sexy mind." In many of her stories, the men were ordinary-
looking, unless her caller wanted it otherwise. No need to
further the myth that sexy men were gorgeous. "Anyway, I
showered, carefully washing all my special places, reveling
in the feel of my bath sponge rubbing my skin. I slipped on
a robe and went to the kitchen to find some breakfast. On
the table, beside the morning paper was another note.

I HOPE YOU'VE FOLLOWED MY INSTRUCTIONS AND
HAVEN'T OPENED THE BOX YET. THE ANTICIPATION IS
MAKING YOU HOT. IS IT?

It sure is, I thought. The note continued:

GOOD. BREAKFAST IS READY FOR YOU. I'LL SEE YOU AT
10:00. AND REMEMBER, NO TOUCHING YOURSELF.

"I found a carefully cut grapefruit half and a bowl of
cereal on the counter, with hot coffee on the warmer. He

was so considerate. I ate my breakfast, unable to concentrate on anything. What was in the box?

"At 8:55 I walked back into the bedroom, fetched the box from the bathroom and put it on the bed. As the digital clock clicked from 8:59 to 9:00 A.M., I opened the red ribbon and tore through the white wrapping paper. I pulled the top off the box and folded back gobs of tissue paper. Then I found a note.

DARLING, IN HERE YOU'LL FIND A NEW TOY I BOUGHT FOR US. INSERT IT, THEN PUT ON THE CLOTHING, AND NOTHING ELSE. WAIT FOR ME IN THE LIVING ROOM. I'LL BE THERE AT TEN. AND NO PLAYING WITH YOURSELF!

"I'm quite the devil, am I not, *cherie*?"

Jacques had gotten into the story as he always did and Alice grinned. She picked up one of the dildos, thought about an item she had seen on the Internet the previous evening, then continued the tale. "I rummaged in the box and found a sizable dildo with a narrow bulge about halfway up and another at the blunt end, and a door with some batteries inside. I tried to find a switch to turn the thing on so I could find out what it did, but there was nothing. Although it was pretty thick around, I knew it would fit inside of my pussy with little coaxing, especially since I was so excited at the sight of that new toy. As I put it aside, I wondered again what the electronic gizmo was for. I reached back into the box and pulled out the clothing, a pair of jeans, a bustier, a sheer blouse, and a pair of soft black slippers. 'There're no underwear,' I said aloud. Then I smiled. 'Fine with me.' "

"Umm. Fine with me too," Jacques said. "Tell me what you looked like. What did you do?"

"I removed my robe and stared at the dildo. Then I slowly

inserted it into my hungry pussy. At that moment I wanted nothing more than to stroke my clit and get myself off, but the note specifically said that I was not to masturbate so I reluctantly removed my fingers from my crotch. As I moved around, I discovered that the dildo stayed in place, tightly inside my cunt, held securely by the bulge in the center. Very little of it stuck out, just enough of the second bulge to keep it from sliding all the way in. I wondered where Jacques found it.

"Slowly, I stood up and put on the bustier. It was a size too small so once it was hooked up the center of the front it squeezed my ribs tightly, lifting my breasts until I almost spilled out the top. I saw that if I positioned my breasts properly my nipples poked through tiny holes. The fullness in my pussy and the tight almost corset-like fit of the bustier combined to keep my heat turned up high."

Jacques sighed. "I know you have beautiful breasts, *cherie*."

"Oh yes, I do," Alice purred. "I pulled on the jeans and found that they, too, were a size too small. I knew that Jacques knew my sizes well, so this must all be calculated to make me hot. It was certainly working. As I wiggled into the jeans I suddenly became aware that the crotch of the pants wasn't sewn closed, just laced with a red ribbon. The jeans were so tight that I had to lie on my back and loosen the ribbon to get the zipper closed. Now, if I spread my thighs, I could see the ends of the ribbon and feel air on my crotch. The dildo was held firmly in place, yet my lips were exposed to the air. Oh, Jacques, you devil."

Jacques's chuckle through the phone was warm and liquid.

Alice stood and pulled down her sweatpants. She stretched out on the bed, aroused and already wet. "I looked at the clock and discovered that is was only nine-thirty. I had thirty minutes to wait and think about

Jacques's arrival home. I hoped that he would pull these clothes off and fuck me senseless, but I knew Jacques well enough to know that this was just the beginning.

"I slipped the sheer blouse on and felt the fabric brush against my fully erect nipples. It was quite an outfit but despite all of the erotic details, it was almost decent. Since my nipples were dark and the blouse was navy blue, no one could really see that I wasn't decently clothed, and, although the ribbon showed, it could have been a decoration, not a covering for my naked crotch. And, of course, no one could know about the dildo.

"I walked into the living room and realized that, as I walked, the dildo shifted slightly inside me. God, I was hot. I wanted to wiggle my hips and touch myself, rub my clit until I came, but still I hesitated. Jacques didn't want me to. So I sat on the sofa and waited.

"At exactly ten, I heard the key in the lock. The door opened and Jacques walked in. He wore jeans, a white cotton sweater, and sneakers. He looked so ordinary. 'Stand up,' he said and I stood. 'God, you're sexy,' he growled, 'and you make me hard.' He unzipped his jeans and his fully erect cock sprang forth. 'Fix this for me,' he said.

"I love sucking him, so I quickly got down on my knees and drew his hard cock into my mouth. I did all the things I know he loves, fondled his balls, tickled his anus, flicked my tongue over the tip of his cock, and it was only moments until he filled my mouth with his come."

"Would you do that for me, *cherie*, if we were together?"

"Of course, Jacques. What would you do for me?"

"I would untie that red ribbon and kiss and suck and lick you until you begged for me. I am very talented, you know."

"I'll bet you are. And the other Jacques was a very clever lover too. Just like you. When I finished with his cock, he said, 'That's better,' and zipped up his pants.

"'Not for me,' I whispered, wanting his hands, his

mouth, his cock to relieve my incredible need.

"'I know but you've got a long day in front of you.'

"I frowned, then slipped my fingers into my crotch. Jacques slapped my hand. Hard. I had known he would and I smiled, enjoying the erotic teasing. 'Bad girl,' he snapped. 'You have to wait.' He started toward the door. 'Come with me.'

"I followed. In the driveway was a small red convertible with the top down. I smiled as I realized that he had rented it for us. He opened the door on my side and I saw that the passenger seat was covered with a furry pad. As I went to slide into the car, he grabbed my wrist. 'Just a minute.' He loosened the ribbon that held the crotch of my jeans together until the sides were widely separated. 'Now sit.'

"The furry pad rubbed against my wet lips and pressed the dildo tightly into my channel. Softly, Jacques said, 'The dildo doesn't hurt, does it?'

"'Well, yes and no,' I answered. 'It makes me really hot and so hungry I would love to jump you, but hurt? Not really.'

"Jacques grinned. 'Good.' He slammed the door and leaned into the open car. 'I don't want you to touch your pussy,' he said, 'so these are for you.' First he fastened a wide leather collar around my neck, then he pulled a pair of connected leather manacles from his back pocket and cuffed my wrists together. Then he took a small padlock and locked the short chain between the cuffs to a large ring on the collar. My hands were now at breast level and I was unable to touch my cunt. He reached in and carefully fastened my seat belt, then walked around and got into the car."

"Oh, *cherie*," Jacques said into the phone. "I can just see you like that. Tell me where you are and I'll run to your house and we can play together for the rest of our lives."

"I'm so sorry, Jacques, but you know that giving out my address or phone number is against the rules."

He sighed long and loud. "I know and I'm so sad."

"I am too," Alice said with a small sigh. "Anyway, we drove into the country, the wind in my hair, the fullness in my pussy. I was in plain sight and people in other cars must have wondered at my unusual position, but for the most part the drive was uneventful and slowly, my body calmed. At about eleven-thirty, Jacques pulled the car to the side of a tree-lined lane and stopped. 'We have a bit farther to go, but I think it's time for you to find out the secret of the dildo,' he said. 'Did you notice the battery opening? Curious? Well, here's the control.' He showed me a small box with several dials. 'Let's see how it feels if I turn this.'

"Suddenly there was a whirring and the dildo began to hum, moving inside of me like something alive. Shards of pleasure shot through me, stabbing from my pussy to my nipples. I moved my hips trying to drive the dildo deeper into my cunt." Alice pulled the crotch of her panties aside and slipped the ridged pink dildo into her pussy. As she pressed, the rings of thicker plastic pushed into her like the vibrating dildo she was creating in her story. "'And this one,' Jacques said, turning another dial. The sensation was like having my pussy channel massaged from the inside. I guessed that the bulge around the girth of the dildo was moving deeper inside of me, then further toward the base of the shaft of the artificial penis. The feeling drove me higher.

"'And this,' he said, finding another dial. The bulge around the base of the dildo moved, rubbing my clit. 'Oh, God,' I cried. 'Don't stop.' My eyes closed and my back arched. I squirmed, confined in my seat belt, unable to get my hands to my crotch. 'You can reach your tits,' he purred, 'so pinch them. And move your hips to make it better.'"

Phone propped against her ear, Alice pulled the dildo out, then pushed it in again. She allowed some of her breathlessness and excitement to flow into the story. "Jacques, can you imagine how it felt? I'm playing with a real dildo now."

"You are? Wonderful. My cock is so big and hard. I wish you were playing with it instead of my hand."

"I wish it, too, Jacques. Tell me, did you make it slippery?"

"Oh, *cherie*. It feels so good. I can picture you with that machine fucking you, so hot waiting for orgasm, just like I am right now."

"Yes, I was. I wanted it, needed it. I sat in the car, parked in the open and rolled my hardened nipples between my fingers, squeezing hard as I tried to drive the dildo more tightly into my pussy. I was higher than I had ever been, hot, swirling colors filling my vision. 'Come for me. Now!' Jacques said, and he reached between my legs and touched my clit. I came, deep, hard spasms of pleasure ricocheting throughout my body, reaching my breasts, my mouth, my cunt. It was as if every muscle in my entire body joined in the pleasure. It went on and on, lasting for long minutes."

"Oh, baby," Jacques said, his accent disappearing as it always did when he came, "damn you're good. Are you fucking yourself with the dildo? Are you close?"

"Yes," Alice whispered.

"Good. Now come for me. I want to hear it."

Alice plunged the dildo into her pussy then, leaving it in place, she rubbed her clit. "Yes," she purred as she rubbed. "Yes."

"Oh, *cherie*," he said, his accent as thick as it had been, "rub your sweet pussy. Touch it and stroke it and think of my big hard cock. Think how it would be if my fingers were stroking you and my cock was filling you."

"Yes," Alice said, feeling the now-familiar pleasures swirling through her. Soon. Just another moment.

"Now I will bite your nipple and you will come, just like you did in that car. I rub, I bite, I fuck you so hard. Come for me, *cherie*."

"Yes!" she shouted as the waves of orgasm pounded through her body. "Yes!"

There were a few moments of silence, then Alice said, "You always do that for me, Jacques."

"And you always do it for me. When I call next time will you tell me about the rest of the day you spent with the dildo in your sweet cunt?"

"Of course. The day had just begun."

"I'll call again soon."

"I hope so."

"You know so."

Chapter 12

At six o'clock Saturday evening Vic picked Alice up at her apartment. "This is lovely," he commented. "So like you, organized and conservative."

Alice wasn't sure she liked that characterization. "You make me sound almost dull."

"Not at all but so unlike Sheherazade. I like you just the way you are, Alice." He looked at her outfit, black linen slacks and a white open-collar shirt with a small tan geometric design. "Yes, I definitely like you just the way you are."

Alice thought about the way Vic saw her. That's the way I was until I started working at Velvet Whispers. Now I'm so much more. I don't want to be conservative Alice Waterman anymore. "Let me get my jacket," she said, leaving Vic in the living room. In the bedroom she peered into her closet. A classic tan linen jacket lay on the bed but suddenly she didn't want to wear it. She flipped through hanger after hanger of basic slacks, blouses, jackets, and vests. How ordinary, she thought.

Then, from the very back of her closet she grabbed a bright red blazer with gold buttons. *I must go to the mall and update my wardrobe.* She found several pins and scattered them on her lapels. Finally, she took a small ladybug pin and attached it to the top of one shoulder. Better. Then she added a bit of mascara and put a coat of red lipstick over the soft coral she had been wearing. Finally she removed the combs that had been controlling her hair and fluffed out her curls. *Conservative indeed. Maybe I want to be a little more like Sheherazade.*

When she arrived back in the living room, Vic had his back to her, gazing at her music collection. "Very eclectic," he said. "Andean, Balkan, country and western, even some Chopin and Mozart. Very nice assortment."

"Thanks," Alice said. "Shall we have dinner?"

He turned and looked at her flame-colored jacket. "Well. Not so conservative after all. You look great."

As it had the previous two dinners, the meal sped by. Conversation roamed from the situation in the Middle East to several new sitcoms on TV. They talked about the unusually warm weather and the possibility of Alice's coming into the city to see Vic's latest video game. When the music began, they danced, Vic holding her at a proper distance. Slowly she moved closer, wanting to feel his body against hers but each time he realized that they were pressed against each other, he backed up. Finally, at about eleven o'clock, they left the restaurant, with Alice aroused and frustrated. She really wanted to crack Vic's uptight facade. They had taken Vic's Buick and, when they arrived back at Alice's apartment, she invited him inside for a nightcap.

"You don't usually drink," Vic said, following Alice into her living room.

"I feel like something silly tonight. Friends and I go out once a week or so and I've gotten quite fond of a concoction made with orange juice, melon liqueur, and vodka. I got the makings recently. Can I interest you in one?"

"Okay. Sure."

Vic followed Alice into the kitchen and watched as she prepared the drinks. "They're called Melon Balls. What do you think?"

Vic sipped. "Delicious," he said downing half the drink as they walked into the living room.

As nice as Vic was being, Alice was becoming impatient with his reluctance to venture into anything even remotely resembling sexuality. She knew he wasn't gay from the stories she had told him. So what was with him?

Vic settled onto the sofa and Alice sat beside him. She touched the rim of her glass to his. "Here's to good sex." *That ought to shake him up a bit,* she thought.

"You mean now?" Vic said, staring.

Alice put her drink down. "Why not?"

"But . . .well . . .I'm not really in your league. I mean . . ."

"Vic, I think there are a few things we should get out into the open. We both know how we met and that's making this really strange. I find you attractive and sexy. This is our third date and I just thought that, since we're here, together, that we might experiment a bit."

"Experiment?"

"See whether we're compatible. Of course, if you don't find me tempting, I will certainly understand."

"Oh, Alice, I find you most tempting. It's just that, well, I'm a bit intimidated."

"I frighten you?"

"No." He paused and stared into his glass. "Sheherazade does."

"I thought we had agreed that she's not real. She's just a character I put on and take off at will."

"I know that, but somehow she's always there, in the back of my mind. I'm sorry."

Alice was somehow amused. "Sheherazade scares the daylights out of you, doesn't she?"

"I'm afraid so." He turned toward her. "Oh, Alice, I've dreamed about making love to you, but in all the dreams, just when we're about to do it, you know, there's Sherry, watching, judging how creative I am. And I always fail. Although I enjoy your stories and have my fantasies, I'm not really very adventurous."

Alice stroked Vic's cheek. "This is all silly. I am who I am and you are who you are. If we're good together, that's great. If not, well nothing's lost."

"A lot is lost. That's what you don't understand. I like you very much. I don't want to sacrifice our friendship. If we go to bed and it's terrible, then what?"

Alice touched her lips to Vic's. "Why should it be terrible?"

"My wife always said that I wasn't much in the bedroom department."

Alice sat back. "There are good and bad lovers, of course. But the bad lovers are the ones with no imagination, no ability to play, to enjoy, and to communicate. We've been communicating and imagining and playing for months on the phone so that shouldn't be a problem."

"On the phone," Vic said. "Not in real life. Face to face. I don't know whether I'm good enough for you. I might disappoint you."

"I really believe, and not from a lot of personal experience, mind you, that couples are good or bad, not individuals. I find you attractive and I'm excited by the possibility of making love with you."

"You want to make love to a basset hound?"

"That's the second time you've used that term. That really bothers you, doesn't it?"

"I guess it does. My wife used that as a term of endearment early in our marriage. Then later, it became her little joke, but eventually I didn't find it funny."

"I can imagine you didn't." Alice put her hand on Vic's

thigh. "Are you going to let her get between us too? There are too many of us here already: you, me, Sheherazade, and now your ex-wife. Let's just be you and me and see what happens."

Vic gazed into Alice's eyes, then his expression softened. "You're right, of course." He put his arms around her and kissed her, putting all the longing he was feeling into the meeting of mouths. Suddenly hunger seemed to sweep over them, ending all of Vic's hesitation. Hands unbuttoned, unbuckled, and unzipped. Mouths quested and found erotic spots, hard flesh, and wetness. "Oh God, baby," he murmured as he paused to unroll a condom over his erection. Then, still on the sofa, he was inside of her. Alice's nails dug into his back while he drove into her. She wrapped her legs around his waist and pulled him closer, bucking her hips to take him more deeply inside her.

Their climaxes were fast and hard. And loud.

"Still think you're a basset hound? I don't know any basset hounds that make love like that."

"It was all right?" Vic asked.

"It was fantastic."

Later they lay on Alice's bed, naked, side by side, sipping drinks. "Do you remember the first story you ever told me?" Vic asked, mellower than she had seen him since they'd first met face to face.

Alice thought. "It was about the toll taker, wasn't it?"

"Yes, and they made love hard and fast like we did. I lived that story a thousand times in my mind, seeing me and you. Remember? Long blond hair and blue eyes?"

Alice grinned. "Not like the real me at all."

"Nor the real me either. But in my fantasies, I was young and virile and you were blond and blue-eyed. You know what? This was much better."

"This was great," Alice said.

"Can I ask you for something really strange? Would you

tell me a story, like Sheherazade used to do? I've always fantasized about being able to touch you while you were telling me one of your wonderful tales."

Alice considered it. Sheherazade was an illusion, a voice on the phone, a figment of her imagination just as surely as her stories were. The real Alice was solid and down to earth. But were they really so separate? Hadn't the gap between her two selves narrowed over the past weeks? She had always believed that she couldn't talk as freely about lovemaking when she could look someone in the eye, but now that Vic had asked, she wanted to tell him a great story. And maybe she could find out what kinds of lovemaking he liked at the same time.

She stood up and padded around the apartment, turning out all the lights. Then, before turning out the small bedside light in the bedroom, she lit several candles, the ones still left from Todd's visit.

She stretched out on the bed and pulled a quilt over the two of them, then cuddled against Vic in the flickering light. "You have to help me," she said. "Close your eyes. Set the scene. Tell me where you are, what you're seeing. Think about the most perfect encounter you can imagine. How would it begin?"

"Boy, you're really asking me to reveal my deepest secrets, aren't you?"

"No. You can create anything you like, so go wherever you want. Let's create people for our story who are gorgeous, perfect creatures who are so sexy that no one can resist us. That's what I imagine when I tell a story."

"You have those fantasies too?"

"Sure. I have long flowing hair. Sometimes it's black, sometimes blond, sometimes red but it's always long and it blows in the wind like a shampoo commercial." She'd shared so many fantasies, but had never been this personal and honest before. She wanted Vic to know that they both had the same insecurities. "I'd have blue eyes with long black lashes, a perfect small nose, and those wonderful full lips that sort of pout, the ones that men find so kissable."

Vic propped himself on one elbow and kissed her softly, nipping at her lower lip. "I think you've got a great, sexy mouth." He lay back down.

"What do you look like in your dreams?"

"I'm tall. I'm always about six foot four, with broad shoulders and lots of muscles. I have black wavy hair and black eyes. I guess you'd say I was a stud, with women panting to get dates with me."

"So you've got all the women you want in your dreams?"

"In my dreams, the one I want most doesn't want me, except on her terms."

"Oh." Alice vaguely remembered that Velvet had told her that Vic liked aggressive women. "She's forceful?"

"Very."

"How do you two meet?" She wanted to hear, and possibly play out Vic's fantasy. "How about at a party? The wine and booze are flowing freely and everyone is feeling quite mellow. Is she there?"

She heard Vic's long-drawn-out, *"Yessss."*

"Does she excite you?"

"Oh yes. I can't take my eyes off of her. She's tall, almost five feet ten and has long red hair that hangs almost to her waist. Her body is firm and trim with small breasts. She isn't wearing the usual party uniform: the slinky dress that advertises her availability. Instead, she's wearing a black blouse buttoned up to her throat and knotted at the waist and tight, black stretch pants. She has accentuated her waist with a silver concho belt, which matches her large silver squash-blossom earrings. She has completed her outfit with knee-high black leather boots that lace up the front with silver rings at the top.

"I start toward her. As I get closer, I admire her green eyes and smooth skin. I gaze at her red lips and feel a further tightening in my pants."

Alice felt Vic take her hand beneath the quilt. As long as Vic was willing to continue the story, Alice was anxious to listen.

"'Hi, gorgeous,' I say, using my most charming voice. 'How about I get you a fresh drink and then we can get to know each other?'

"The girl looks at me. Her eyes roam my body, making me a bit self-conscious. Then she looks away.

"I want to get to know her, then take her to bed even." Vic chuckled. "Actually I don't care if I ever get to know her, I merely want to fuck her senseless, lose myself in her body."

"I'll bet it's not going to be as easy as you think," Alice said.

"No, it's not," Vic said, squeezing her hand. "You know, this storytelling isn't as easy as I thought. It's a bit scary, like I'm telling you all about me."

"I know. If anyone listens to my stories they will find out all the things that turn me on. I can't invent a really good erotic fantasy about activities that don't get me excited." She paused. "You really don't have to make it so personal if you don't want to," Alice said. "We can certainly tell this story other, less scary ways."

"I know, but it's a sort of delicious-scary. I'd like to continue as long as I can." He took a deep breath. "So I say to the woman, 'I'm sorry. Are you with someone?'

"'No,' she says with her back to me.

"'Then why not me?' I ask.

"'You're not my type,' she says.

"Well, I am surprised. 'And what is your type?' I ask.

"She turns and looks at me. 'My type always waits for me to make the first move. As a matter of fact, my type always waits for me to make every move.' "

Alice felt his grip tighten and knew he was telling her something he wanted her to hear, something he'd probably never told anyone. In his fantasy the woman is the aggressor and he is the follower. "I'll bet that gets to you, makes you hard."

"Oh yes, it does," Vic said. "My whole body shudders and I can hardly control my excitement. My pulse is hammering and I'm panting. I can hardly get the words out. 'W-w-what would your type do right now?' I stammer."

Alice leaned close to his ear and whispered, "What does she say?"

"She smiles and says, 'My type would light a cigarette and hand it to me,' so I take out a cigarette, light it, and hand it to her with shaking fingers.

"'Hmm,' she says. 'Very good,' then she just wanders off through the crowd."

Alice held his hand tightly. "I'll bet she comes back. I would, if I were her. I like men who know how to behave and you knew exactly what to do." She heard the hiss of Vic's indrawn breath. She wanted to make him hotter, make it easier for him to talk, she realized, and she'd read enough stories to understand what he would like. "You were such a good boy."

"I was? Oh yes. Well eventually she does come back, almost an hour later. I stare at her, but she says, sternly, 'Never look me in the eye. You may only look at me from the shoulders down unless I give you permission. Understand?'

"I looked at her shiny boots, staring at the sharply pointed toes, the heavy silver rings through the zippers, and the high spike heels. 'Yes, I understand.' I can hardly speak."

"What's her name?" Alice whispered. "We can call her anything you want."

"Valerie," Vic said. "She says that her name is Valerie. 'You must learn to say, *Yes, Valerie,* or *Yes, ma'am.* Now practice that.'

"'Yes, Valerie,' I say. 'Yes, ma'am.'

"'Not bad for a beginner,' she says. As she speaks, I watch her hands with those long red fingernails that are sliding up and down the hips of her tight pants. 'Now go into the bathroom,' she says. Her voice is soft but firm and seems to brook no objections. 'Take off your shorts and bring them to me. Quickly, with no dawdling.'

"God, I'm so hot." Vic hesitated, so Alice said, "I'll bet you're a good boy and do as you're told?"

"Oh yes, I do. I almost run into the bathroom, pull off my slacks and shorts and allow my huge erection to poke from the front of my crotch. I want to touch it, rub it, but I know she's waiting, so I pull my slacks back on, ball my shorts in my hand and hurry back through the crowd. I find her where I left her, standing beside the bar. I remember and gaze down at her boots, as I surreptitiously hand her my shorts. Valerie props her elbow on the bar as she dangles my shorts from her index finger for all to see. There are several snickers from other people at the party but I'm willing to risk anything. I start to reach for the shorts but Valerie glares at me. I drop my hand and blush for the first time in years, lowering my eyes to her leather boots."

"You were being such an obedient boy," Alice says, still holding his hand, using his grip as an indication of his excitement. "I like obedient boys."

"What would you say now?" Vic asked, his voice hoarse, his need evident.

Picking up the story, Alice continued, "I would be very glad that you did as you were told. I find you quite attractive and you would be a good addition to my collection. 'I see we understand each other,' I would say. 'Go and find my coat. It's long, black leather. Bring it to me and we'll get out of here.' Will you do that, Vic?"

"Yes. Of course. I go into the bedroom and root through the coats. I find hers, then I stop for a moment and wonder why I'm doing this. Has this girl cast some kind of spell over me? She has and I know it. And I don't care. I have to have her. I will do anything she wants just to get a chance to make love to her."

Alice shifted her grip to his wrist and held it tightly. She recalled Todd's commanding tone and trembled. She knew just how Vic was feeling, wanting to be controlled by an erotic fantasy woman. She wanted Vic to continue so she said, "Tell me what happens then."

"Well, later, in the cab on the way to her apartment, she says, 'Give me your wrists.' She pulls a length of soft black rope from her purse and stares at me. I know what she wants, so I offer her my wrists and she ties them together, then reaches down and lifts the heavy silver ring that's attached to one of her boots. She takes the free end of the rope and ties it to the ring.

"When we reach our destination, the rope forces me to get out of the taxi carefully and walk bent over with my head level with her breasts. Twice, I almost stumble when Valerie takes a particularly long step." Vic hesitated.

"Tell me," Alice urged.

"This is really kinky but when I regain my balance, she laughs and I'm so aroused by her laughter that I think I'll come right there. Am I perverted, Alice?"

"Not at all. I think it's really hot," Alice said. "Does she take you to her apartment?"

"Yes. We enter her apartment and she turns on the lights. All the furniture is chrome, glass, or black lacquer. The rug is dark red with deep pile and it silences our footsteps.

"Without a word she unties the end of the rope attached to her boot and reties it to a ring embedded in the wall. Then she turns and disappears into the next room. It's very warm in her apartment so, since I'm still wearing my winter jacket, I begin to sweat and feel a trickle of perspiration run down my side. I wiggle as much as I can, trying to brush my shirt against the tiny river.

"'Don't squirm!' she snaps as she reenters the room. She has changed into a black corset that reveals her full breasts and pussy and she has put on long black gloves without fingers. She has also pulled her hair back tightly and wound it into a tight knot at the back of her neck. She's still wearing her boots and is banging a short riding crop against the top of one. God, this is really hard to talk about."

"Your story is really getting me hot." Alice took Vic's hand and placed it on her mound. His fingers slipped naturally between her lips and she knew he could feel her wetness. She didn't know whether she could actually become the character in Vic's story and play the scene out with him, but the tale was making her hungry. Now she understood exactly what her callers felt when she spun one of her fantasies. "Tell me what happens then," Alice said, an air of command in her voice.

"Valerie flicks the crop against the back of my thigh," Vic continued. "The effect is muffled by my jeans but the crop still stings. 'You were looking at me,' she snaps. I immediately drop my gaze.

"Valerie reaches up, unties my hands, and unfastens the rope from the wall. As she stretches, her naked breasts brush against me. I wonder how much of this I can take before I come in my pants."

Alice placed her hand gently over Vic's extremely hard cock. "Go on," she said, squeezing. She can hear Vic's hoarse, quick breathing and feel his body shake.

"Valerie walks over to the sofa and sits down, the rope still in her hands. 'Strip,' she orders. I obey as quickly as I can with my hands shaking as hard as they are.

"I stand before her, naked. Her eyes roam over my body, my erection poking straight in front of me, aching for relief.

"'I demand stamina from my men,' she says. 'You may not come unless I give you permission. The first time is always the most difficult so I will give you some help. Crawl over here.'

"I do it, on my hands and knees. I'll do anything she wants. 'Stand up straight,' she says, 'and touch yourself.' I have never masturbated with anyone watching so I hesitate.

The crop swishes through the air again and lands on my right ass cheek. It stings but it also heightens my awareness of my body and its needs. I reach out and wrap my hand around my huge cock."

Alice took Vic's hand and placed it on his cock. "Ohh," he groaned, trying to pull his hand away, but Alice placed her hand on top of his and urged him to keep it there. "Keep it there," she said, "just like in the story."

"Yes, ma'am." He kept his hand around his cock as he was doing in the fantasy.

"'Stroke it until you come,' Valerie says. 'Then you can serve me properly.' "

"Yes," Alice whispered, "do that for me. I want to feel your hand move."

As he continued the story, Vic's hand slowly moved over his erection. "Valerie settles back and stares at my hand.

"I am very embarrassed but also very excited. I squeeze my cock and run my fingers up and down it." With Alice's hand on top of his, Vic's hand moved faster as he lost himself in his fantasy. "Oh God, Alice, oh God." It was only a moment until he spurted all over her legs. "I'm so sorry," Vic said. "I don't know what came over me."

"I do, and it pleases me very much. The power of the images you created was erotic as hell and drove you over the edge." She handed Vic several tissues and he cleaned himself up quickly.

"I've never done that with a woman," Vic said.

"Why not? It was wonderful."

"What about you? You haven't come."

Alice placed his hand on her pussy. "Fix it! Touch me!" She felt his body react to the command in her voice. His fingers worked, rubbing her clit. She grabbed the back of his neck and pushed his face against her breast. "Suck!" Quickly, his mouth and teeth drove her upward as his fingers played her pussy like a fine instrument. He seemed to know when to stroke softly and when to press hard. "Good boy, don't stop." He slipped two fingers inside of her and found a spot that made her body jerk with erotic pleasure when he pressed. "Very good. You serve me well."

He continued to fuck her with his fingers, then slid down and took her clit between his lips and sucked. She tried to hold back, wanting the wonderful sensations he was creating to last, but she was unable to prevent the waves of erotic pleasure from engulfing her. Suddenly the orgasm burst through her clenched muscles, and lasted several minutes.

Later, Vic said, "I asked you to tell me a story and I ended up telling you my deepest secrets. You must be a witch."

They dozed and, after making love once more, Vic said, "I think I'd better go home."

"You can stay if you want," Alice said, barely able to stay awake.

"I know, but I'd prefer to head home. It's almost morning and I have a lot of thinking to do. I want to take some time alone to consider what we did tonight."

"I could order you to stay," Alice said, unsure of where Vic's head was.

"Yes, you could, and that's what I have to think about. It's really unnerving to find out that you're not the basset hound you always thought you were."

"You're no basset hound. That's for sure." Alice yawned.

"I'll call you tomorrow. Actually today. Okay?"

Still a bit insecure, she thought, even after all that they had shared. "I'll look forward to hearing from you." As she heard him close the front door behind him, she burrowed beneath her covers and slept soundly.

Chapter 13

After their first sexual encounter, Alice and Vic dated almost every weekend. There were a few repeats of the dominant games they had played, but for the most part, the sex was good, hot, and traditional. In addition, through the summer Alice continued both of her jobs working at Dr. Tannenbaum's office and taking calls three evenings. She also visited her mother at least once a week and tried to join Betsy and Velvet for girls' night out. The three women became, if possible, even closer. When the doctor's office closed for two weeks in August, Alice and Vic spent a week driving around the south, enjoying sightseeing by day and playing in motel bedrooms by night. She also dated several other men, two of whom she met through Velvet Whispers and three who were introduced to her by her two best friends. Some of these dates resulted in more dates, a few ended after one evening.

In early September, Mrs. Waterman went to sleep one evening and died quietly before morning. Although it was sad, both Alice and her sister agreed that their mother's death was peaceful and she was now beyond the pain that had begun to debilitate her. Without the drain of nursing-home payments, Alice had a newfound financial freedom, and had some serious decisions to make. She knew that she was exhausted, burning the candle at more than two ends. She needed to simplify her life but she wasn't sure how. Should she give up Velvet Whispers? That seemed the most logical thing to do.

Maybe she should tell her callers that she was taking a vacation and that Velvet would be in touch when she was ready to take calls again. Yes, she should do that.

The following evening, a regular client named Hector was her first caller. "Hi, Sherry," he said. "Got a story for me tonight? Tell me a really hot one. It's been a long, tough week." She knew the kind of stories he liked and tonight she was going to tell him a doozie. One last present for him before she retired.

"Sure thing, sweetness," Alice said in her Sheherazade voice. "It's about a night when I was very naughty."

"Tell me."

"Well, several years ago I took a job waiting tables at a place called La Contessa. I was good at my job and I liked the work, not as much as I like talking to you, but that was before. Anyway, I got as many huge tippers as I got nasty customers so it was okay." Alice laughed, remembering her short stint as a waitress just after Ralph split. "I remember the man who slipped me a thirty-dollar tip for a sixty-dollar dinner check and one who yelled at me for fifteen minutes for delivering his steak too rare."

"Yeah, I'll bet," Hector said. "I always try to be nice to waitresses. My ex-wife used to wait tables and I remember the stories she used to tell."

"I don't think your ex-wife had any experiences like this one and she probably never had a customer like this guy. I know I never had. The man was not really good-looking, but he had a sensuality that was almost palpable. He wore his ebony hair long so you just wanted to run your fingers through it. His eyes were the blue of glacial ice, yet they also seemed warm and inviting. He wore a tight black turtleneck that fit his body like a second skin with long tight cuffs that almost caressed his wrists. His black jeans were, if possible, tighter than his shirt, his boots were black with silver studs and toe tips. His only jewelry was a silver hoop in one ear."

"Sounds like quite a stud."

"He was. I spotted him as he stood waiting to be seated. Although I tried not to stare, I found myself unable to move. I wondered whether he was meeting someone." Alice's breathing quickened just thinking about the man in black she was creating and she knew her excitement would add to Hector's enjoyment. "Well, the host sat him in my section. In the corner at table thirty-five. 'Good evening,' I said in my best waitress voice. 'My name is Sherry and I'll be serving you this evening. May I get you a drink?'

"His eyes met mine and our gazes locked. He stared at me, then his eyes caressed my body from my neck to my toes. You see the outfits we wore were quite revealing. Very low-cut peasant blouses and full, red-print skirts.

"He stared, then said, 'Yes, of course. I'll have a glass of sangria, Sherry.'

"I saw that the host had put only one menu on the table so I asked, 'Will you be dining alone?'

"'Alas, yes,' he said, still staring into my eyes. 'I have set my last lover free and I'm looking for another. Are you available?' "

"Whoa," Hector said. "He was really something. Set his last lover free. What did that mean?"

"I wondered about that myself, but he kept staring at me

and I found that my knees began to tremble and my brain locked up tight. I couldn't concentrate. Was he asking me out? Several customers had done that over the months, and, although there was no strict rule against dating patrons, I had always said no. 'I'm sorry,' I answered, 'but no.' "

"I'll bet he was sorry too. I know just how he must have felt," Hector said. "How often have I gotten that same answer from you?"

Alice laughed. "Lots. But don't stop trying. It's good for my ego and sometime I might just say yes." Alice knew Hector lived in the New York area and maybe, with more time on her hands, she would agree to meet him. What did she have to lose? She dragged her thoughts back to her story. "So the man in black said, 'That's a shame.'

"I cleared my throat," Alice continued, "then said, 'I'll get your sangria while you decide what to order.' As I walked toward the bar's service area, I could feel his eyes on me. My knees shook and I could feel the wetness between my legs. He was the sexiest man I'd ever seen and there was something more. Something deeply, darkly erotic.

"When I returned with the man's drink, my hands shook so much that, as I placed the glass on the table, several drops of the blood-red liquid fell on his pants. 'I'm t-t-terribly s-s-sorry,' I stammered. I grabbed a napkin from a nearby table and dabbed at the almost-invisible stain.

"The hand that snapped around my wrist was like a vise. 'That was very careless,' the man said softly. Then he smiled. 'You really should be punished for your clumsiness.' "

"He really said that?" Hector asked, his breathing a bit faster.

Alice caught Hector's reaction. He was as excited at the way the story was unfolding as she was. Interesting. "Yes, he said *punished*. I wondered why he had said that? Would he punish me? How? Oh God. I swallowed hard.

"'That excites you, doesn't it?' the man purred. 'I can feel your pulse race.' "

"Does that idea excite you, Sherry?" Hector asked, his voice filled with longing. "God, I'd love to do bad things to you."

"Let's finish the story, sweetness, then we can talk." She heard Hector's breath catch. She was definitely tempted. "So there I was, with him holding my wrist, telling me how excited I was getting. Well I couldn't speak. All my life I had had fantasies of someone controlling me, spanking me, loving me." *Did I really have such fantasies?* Alice wondered. "Although I had had a few lovers, I had never shared my dark desires with any of them. They were too kinky. Too black. Yet here he was, a man who seemed to know my deepest wishes. Or was it just an accident. 'I'm sorry, sir,' I said, taking a deep breath. 'Can I take your dinner order?' *That's good,* I thought. *Fall back on the familiar routine.* But he was still holding my wrist."

"I know these are just stories," Hector said, "but they make me so hot. Do you really have those fantasies, Sherry? Do you really want someone to take over like that? Control you?"

What could she say? She had never thought about this kind of sex play happening to her until that weekend with Todd. It had always been just a story. Now it was becoming much more. She returned to her tale. "'Your pulse is still pounding,' the man in black whispered. 'We'll continue this later.' I wondered what he meant, but I concentrated on my job.

"I took his dinner order and tried to involve myself in caring for the other diners. When his order was up, I put the plates on my tray and served him calmly and efficiently. Or at least I tried to be calm. Tried to sound calm. His expression told me he wasn't fooled.

"As I waited on other tables, I frequently looked at him, and each time I glanced in his direction, I found his eyes on me. It wasn't just a coincidence. It felt like he was seducing me with his gaze. It was almost half an hour later when I returned to his table to retrieve his empty plates.

"'That was delicious,' he said, his voice little more than a purr, 'but not totally satisfying. I need something hot for dessert. Any suggestions?'

"Me, I wanted to say. Instead I murmured, 'We have a wonderful hot apple cobbler.'

"The man looked at his watch, hidden beneath the long sleeve of his black shirt. 'It's almost nine-thirty. What time do you finish here?'

"I cleared my throat. 'I do recommend the apple cobbler.'

"'You want this. I know you understand that you deserve what I have for you, and I also know you crave it. You are telling me that with every fiber of your being. I can read you like a book and I know exactly what you want.' "

Alice could hear Hector's heavy breathing and knew her story was having the desired effect. She also knew that her body was responding too. Fortunately she had changed into an old sweat suit after work so she rubbed her aching nipples as she continued.

"Again I swallowed and tried not to let my voice squeak. 'And what, exactly, do you think I want?'

"'You want to be punished for spilling my drink. You want me to restrain you, then spank you like the naughty girl you are. You want the feeling of surrendering to me.' "
The idea of spanking appealed to Alice when she had read a story the previous week. Now it just became part of the fantasy she was creating. Did she want something like this to happen?

"I wish I could be like that guy," Hector said wistfully. "I'd love to dominate a woman like that, but I'm too much of a chicken to ever do it for real."

"Are you really?" Alice asked, then didn't wait for an answer. "Well, you'll never guess what happened next. I was standing close to the man's chair and my skirt covered his movements. Suddenly his hand was between my thighs, his fingers touching my panties. 'You want this like you've never wanted anything else. You're hot and wet and you can barely keep your thighs together.'

"He knew me too well. Much too well. Then the hand was gone. 'I get off at eleven.' I had said it, committed myself to him and to whatever he wanted from me.

"'I drive a black BMW,' he said. 'It will be parked by the back door at eleven and I will wait for fifteen minutes. Be there or regret it all your life.' "

"Did you go?" Hector asked.

"Well, silently I took his credit card and returned with the charge slip. I knew I was blushing and I could barely keep my hands from shaking. He signed and as he stood to leave, he leaned close and whispered, 'For you, my love, I might wait until eleven-thirty. Please don't disappoint us both.'

"Then he was gone. I spent the remainder of my shift in a daze. I took orders, served food and alcohol, but my mind was on the man with the BMW. Could I trust him? Could he fulfill my fantasies? Yes, I admitted to myself, to both questions."

"Wow," Hector whispered.

"It's been more than fifteen minutes, Hector," Alice said glancing at the clock. "Shall I continue?"

"Hell yes," Hector said. "Tell me the rest."

"At eleven-fifteen I walked out of La Contessa, my nipples tight and aching, my pussy soaked, my body craving what was to come. I spotted the BMW immediately, opened the passenger door, and slipped inside.

"'I'm glad you came,' the man said. 'I would have been quite sad had you not appeared.'

"'I think I would have been too,' I whispered."

"Me too," Hector said with a laugh.

"'Good girl,' he said, sounding genuinely pleased. He

reached around my waist, grabbed the seat belt and pulled it across my body. Since it was a warm midsummer evening, I hadn't worn anything over my blouse. 'Now we have some rules to agree to. Can you snap your fingers?'

"Strange request, I thought, but I snapped. 'Good,' he said. 'If you snap your fingers or say the word *marshmallow*, I will stop whatever I'm doing. Do you understand and agree?'

"'Yes.'

"'You will call me Sir. Nothing more, and nothing less. Do you understand?'

"'Yes, Sir.'

"'Excellent.' With deft fingers, the man untied the string that held the top of my blouse. The tie loosened and he pulled the top down so my bra-covered breasts were exposed. He withdrew a small pair of scissors from a compartment in his door and quickly cut the straps of my bra. It took only a moment before the bra was gone, my breasts free, the strap of the shoulder harness cold against the skin between them. My nipples were already swollen, but he pinched the turgid tips until they were aching. Then he took two small suction devices and fastened them to my tits, causing almost painful pressure. Almost painful, but not quite. It was like two mouths sucking on my breasts as hard as they could."

Alice moved her hand down her belly and slid her fingers beneath the waist of her sweatpants. She found her pussy already wet from the images imprinted on her brain.

"'Put your hands on your hips,' he said, softly but firmly, 'and don't move them. Close your eyes and think about your tits. Think about the pressure, the almost-pain and the cool wind against your skin. Think that anyone who looks carefully will know what your breasts are feeling and think about how hot this makes you. I want your tits and your mind at their most sensitive when we get to our destination. It won't take long.'

"'Yes, Sir,' I said, placing my palms against my hipbones and closing my eyes.

"We drove for only about five minutes, then I felt the car slow, turn, and stop. I heard a garage door open and the car move forward and the door close again. 'We're here,' he said.

"I opened my eyes to what had obviously been a two-car garage once. Now half of the structure was walled off. I got out of the car, the sucking devices making every move pleasure and torture. My large breasts swayed as I walked propelled by his hand in the small of my back.

"We walked through a doorway into the other half of the garage and I gasped. The room was paneled in dark wood, with a thick cream-colored carpet cushioning my steps. There were mirrors on one entire wall and the ceiling. In the center of the room there was a large X-shaped wooden frame that stood about six feet tall and was about three feet wide at the ends of the arms. In the corner was an armless desk chair. 'First,' he said, 'snap your fingers.'

"I did, remembering that I was to snap if I got into trouble. 'I understand, Sir,' I said.

"He led me over to the chair, sat in it and quickly removed all of my clothes, leaving the suction devices on my breasts. Then he pulled at one wrist and I tumbled across his lap. 'You were very clumsy earlier,' he said, his voice soft and oily. 'You deserve more than this, but I will go easy for our first time.' "

"He was going to spank you?" Hector asked. "Man, oh man."

I wondered how the story had gotten to this, but it was obviously where Hector and I wanted it to go. "Oh yes," I said. "He was going to punish me for my clumsiness."

"And you let him?"

"I not only let him, I wanted it."

"Man," Hector said, "I can see it and feel it."

"I had no time to wonder as his palm slapped my ass

cheek. I felt the sting in my tender nether parts, but it was just a sting. The second slap merely stung a bit more, but by the fifth, the sting had become pain and my entire backside was tender. Then he stopped."

"Did it hurt?" Hector asked. "My cock's all hard just thinking about it."

"Oh yes. But I was surprised that the pain was also pleasure. I was so wet and hot." Alice's fingers were rubbing her clit and she knew she was close to coming.

"Tell me more," Hector said.

"'You enjoyed that. You have discovered the pleasure in a little pain.' The man caressed my ass cheeks tenderly. Then his fingers slipped into my slit. It was sopping. 'Oh yes,' he said, laughing. 'You liked this a lot.' His fingers penetrated deep into my cunt and his thumb rubbed my clit. I climaxed, my entire body quaking as the spasms took me. 'Oh my God. Good. So good,' I cried.

"'My dear, you're perfect,' he said, still gently rubbing my pussy lips as I came down from the strongest orgasm I remembered. I knew from the moment I saw you that you could be a most wonderful playmate. I would like to do so many things with you, teach you so much about your own sensuality. Would you like that?'

"I could barely get the words out. 'Oh yes, Sir.'

"The man unzipped the fly of his jeans and pulled out his swollen cock. See how excited you make me?'"

"Oh, Sherry, you make me crazy too," Hector said. "I'm going to come soon."

"That's wonderful," Alice said. "Remembering that night is making me hot too." She rubbed her pussy, almost over the edge. "So I gazed at the man's cock, then into his eyes. He nodded and I knelt between his spread knees. I took the nob into my mouth, licked and sucked at the tip, then my mouth engulfed the entire staff. Deep in my throat

I worked the base of my tongue and my cheeks, trying to give him as much pleasure as he had given me. When I cupped his balls through his jeans, he climaxed and I swallowed every drop." Alice came then, but managed to keep telling the story. "When his cock was flaccid again, I sat back on my haunches and gazed at his face. He wore an expression of pure joy, an expression I had helped put there.

"'That was beautiful,' he said softly.

"I couldn't speak.

"'Do you see that frame over there?' he asked as he removed the suckers on my tits.

"'Yes, Sir,' I said.

"'If you come here after work tomorrow night, I will tie you to that, arms spread wide over your head, legs tied far apart so I can play with your pussy at my leisure.'"

Hector gasped and I knew he was coming, but I finished my tale anyway.

"I looked, first at the frame, then at the man who had awakened so much in me.

"'And we can make love in so many ways.' He lifted my face and kissed me gently on the lips. 'Please,' he said, passion and desire in his eyes. 'I want you so much. Climb into my car each night and I will show you so much, and share pleasure you have only dreamed of.'

"'I'll be there,' I said. 'Yes, I'll be there.' "

Alice heard Hector's long sigh. "That was a wonderful story. Did you meet him the next night?"

"Yes," Alice said softly, removing her hand from between her legs.

"Will you tell me about that night next time I call?" Wasn't she going to tell him that she was retiring? One more call. What would it hurt?

"Of course, Hector."

"Next week? Monday? Same time?"

"Sure. It's a date, sweetness."

"Great, then I'll talk to you then. Will you also think about going out with me sometime? We could meet and, well, explore."

"I'll think about it."

Still unsure what she was going to do, she hung up.

Chapter 14

That Saturday night, Alice and Vic spent the evening in the city at a small club in Greenwich Village, listening to jazz. Afterward, they went back to Vic's apartment and made love. She stayed over and the following morning, they went to brunch at a trendy local restaurant. "I'm thinking about leaving Velvet Whispers," she said, sipping orange juice and champagne.

"You really should. You don't need that stuff anymore. I've been telling you that you've been doing too much and I've given it a lot of thought. I think you should marry me. Then you can give up the phone business, quit your dentist job, and move in with me." As Alice watched, Vic began to talk faster and faster. "I'm very well-off, so we could travel. See the world. I've been doing more thinking about that X-rated game I talked to you about too. We could do it together. I could pay you as a consultant if you want."

When he paused for breath, Alice put her hand on his. "You sound like you've got it all planned."

"I have. It will work. We're good together, in and out of bed."

"Vic, you know I care for you, but have you listened to yourself? You're talking like a pitchman. Who are you trying to sell, me or you? You talk about all the reasons we should get married except the most important one. You haven't mentioned love once."

"Of course I love you. That goes without saying."

"No, it doesn't and you didn't say it because it's not the most important element of your thinking. Maybe it's there between us, I don't know." Alice was sorting things out as she spoke, and she found she was seeing things more clearly. "I do know that I'm not ready to settle down yet."

"Oh, Alice, I just want to make you happy."

"I love spending time with you and I don't want that to stop but I have a few other men I date and I don't want that to stop either." When Vic looked dejected, she continued, "I can't be exclusive with you. Not yet, maybe not ever, but does that really change the good times we have?"

"I guess not, but I hate the thought of sharing you."

"I know and I'm sorry that it makes you unhappy, but I've got to have time to decide what I want. I've never had that luxury before. First I had my parents making my decisions, then Ralph. I spent a lot of years after Ralph left in limbo, drifting, then I had my mother's illness. Now I'm free to do whatever I want, and I need time to figure out what that is. I hope you can accept that."

Vic took Alice's hand across the table. "As long as I can spend time with you and you're happy, it's great. You're really going to leave Velvet Whispers?"

"I think so. It's the logical thing to eliminate. It takes up my evenings and keeps me up much later than I really want.

One night last week I was up until almost one."

"Good. I hate to think of you on those sleazy phone calls."

"You didn't think they were sleazy when you were calling me."

"That's different."

Alice raised an eyebrow. "Is it?"

"I don't know, but I'm happy you're leaving."

The idea of leaving Velvet Whispers is logical, Alice thought. *Why then does it make me so sad?* Changing the subject, Alice asked, "Did you mean what you said about the video game?"

"You mean about you helping me? Absolutely. I've got dozens of ideas for it and you'd be just the person to write the scripts."

"I think that would be a gas. Between my stories and your computer skills, we'd make one hell of an adventure game." And if she left Velvet Whispers she would have her evenings, all day on Wednesdays, and the weekends to go into the city and work with Vic. It was entirely logical.

Vic squeezed her hand. "Just tell me that you'll occasionally think about marrying me. Maybe you'll change your mind."

That afternoon, after she arrived home, Alice phoned Velvet and told her of her decision to leave Velvet Whispers. "Are you sure that's what you want to do?" Velvet asked. "I know how much you enjoy your calls and we will all miss you if you leave. You have quite a group of regulars and they will be really upset."

"I know, but it's the logical thing to do. I'll stay with Dr. Tannenbaum and keep the medical coverage and all, and Vic has asked me to work with him on his computer game."

"Oh, honey, I know that you have to make your own decisions but I just don't want to lose you, as an employee or as a friend."

"Oh, Velvet. We won't lose each other. The three of us can still have girls' night out. That will be just like it always has been."

"Shall I take you out of the computer? I won't tell any of your regulars yet. Maybe you'll change your mind."

"I don't think so. Hector is calling tomorrow night and he'll be my last caller."

"I can see I'm in for lots of disappointed men."

After she hung up with Velvet, Alice called Betsy and told her the same thing and, as she had expected, she got the identical reaction. Betsy, however, was more forceful in her suggestion that leaving wasn't necessarily the best idea. "I know it's the logical thing to do," Betsy said, "but I think you're nuts."

Through the day on Monday, Alice thought about her twin conversations. Was this really the right thing? Talking with Vic the day before, it had seemed so simple. Was it really?

That evening, Hector called precisely at eight. "You're right on time, Hector," she said.

"I'm really anxious to hear what happened to you and that guy the next night."

Alice settled onto her bed, Roger beside her. Was this going to be her last call? She could take some time, of course, and taper off, but cold turkey was the best. Well, she'd go out in a blaze of glory. "His name was Daniel. I had learned that as he drove me home after our wonderful night together. Daniel. I couldn't imagine anyone calling him Dan or Danny. I couldn't imagine myself calling him Daniel. He was just Sir.

"I arrived at La Contessa at the regular time the following evening and went through the motions of setting up for the dinner crowd. Would he be here? Would he eat at the restaurant? Would he be waiting at the back door in his BMW?

"The evening crawled by. I looked at my watch and it was six o'clock. An hour later it was only six-fifteen. It took weeks for it to become eight o'clock and decades until ten-thirty. And always my eyes scanned the incoming diners. He wasn't among them. I poured coffee for a customer, brought a check to another, all in a daze. Several times the maitre d' had to remind me to give a customer the dessert menu or refill a water glass. But I was barely functioning. He would be waiting for me outside. He had to be.

"He had given me an instruction. 'Wear no underpants,' he had told me, 'so that every time your thighs brush together and rub against your pussy, you'll think of me.' As if I could think about anything else. Would he be there? Please, be there.

"When my shift was over I grabbed my purse and ran out the rear door. I looked around the back parking lot. His car wasn't there. *Oh God,* I thought. *He isn't coming.* I looked at my watch. Five minutes to eleven. It was still early. My breathing was rapid and my hands shook. I fumbled in my purse, found my car keys and opened my car door. I'd sit in my car and wait for him. He would come."

"He did come, didn't he?" Hector asked.

"Oh yes. 'Leave your purse in the car,' a voice said from behind my shoulder. 'You won't need it.'

"I closed my eyes and took a deep breath. He had come for me after all. 'Yes, Sir,' I whispered. I put my purse under the front seat and locked the car door. Still behind me, he took the keys from my trembling hand. Then he pressed his body against mine, trapping my chest against my car's closed door. He reached around my hips and his hand quickly burrowed beneath my full flowered skirt, his fingers dipping into my sopping cunt. 'Good girl,' he said. 'You did as I asked.'

"Asked, told, demanded, it was all the same. And I couldn't do anything else. I nodded.

"'Remember last night and those suckers on your tits? Well tonight I want all your concentration between your legs.' He maneuvered a harness of some kind around my hips beneath my skirt and hooked it in place. It was soft leather, held together with cold steel rings and bits of chain. 'Spread your legs wide,' he said, still pressing me against the car with his chest.

"When my legs were spread, he bit my earlobe, just hard enough to cause me pain. 'I said wide,' he growled. I widened my stance.

"'Now hold very still and don't move.' He released the pressure against my back. For a moment I considered how this would look to someone coming out of the back door of the restaurant. I was leaning against the side of my car, with a man laying his hands all over me. What would someone think? I didn't care.

"He lifted the back of my skirt and I felt cool air against the backs of my thighs. I jumped when I felt something cold against my hot pussy lips. 'I said stand still,' he hissed.

"'I'm sorry, Sir. You just surprised me.'

"'Nothing I do, nothing we do, should surprise you,' he said, chuckling."

Alice thought about the candle Todd had used to fuck her, then continued. "'True,' I whispered, as much to myself as to him. Suddenly I was filled. My pussy lips were stretched and my passage was as full as it had ever been. A huge dildo was being pushed deep inside me. Relentlessly filling, stretching, demanding. I felt him push the rod in deeper and deeper until I knew I could take no more, yet he kept filling me. Then he stopped and I felt a strip of something pulled down my belly, between my legs, and up between my cheeks to fasten to the harness in the back. As he pulled the strap tighter, the dildo pressed even more tightly inside me.

"He quickly pulled my blouse down in the front and, with a deft flip, my breasts were out of the cups of my bra. He leaned against me, forcing my engorged nipples against the cold metal of the car. 'You're so hot you'll come with almost nothing more from me, won't you?'

"'Yes, Sir,' I said, barely able to stand, barely able to breathe.

"'We can't have you this high all evening, so I'll let you come now.' His small laugh warmed my ear. 'Let's see whether you're so high that you can come without me even touching you. Feel that artificial cock fill your cunt. Feel your hot, hard nipples against the cold window. Are you close?'

"'Yes,' I groaned.

"'How close? How close to grasping that dildo with your pussy and squeezing it, coming against it.'

"'Very.'

"'Let's measure,' he said into my ear. 'If ten is climax, where are you?'

"'Nine point nine,' I said without thinking."

Hector laughed. "Sherry, I'm at about nine point five right now."

"Don't come too fast, Hector," Alice said. "This story has a long way to go, if you want it to."

"Oh, I do."

"Then the man I called Sir licked the back of my neck, then bit the nape. 'Tell me.'

"'Nine point nine nine,' I said, barely able to speak.

"He pressed his hips against my buttocks and moved so the strap shifted the dildo inside of me. Then he pressed the tip of his tongue into my ear and fucked my ear with it. 'Tell me.'

"'Oh God,' I groaned. 'Oh God.'

"He bit my earlobe hard and I climaxed. I couldn't help it. He hadn't touched me with his hands but I was coming anyway. Hard, hot, fast, my pussy spasming against the huge dildo in my cunt. 'Yessss,' I hissed.

"'God, you're wonderful,' he said, slowly releasing the pressure of his body that forced me against the cold car, turning me around so I saw him for the first time. Tears filled my eyes as I looked at his face, warm and inviting, his eyes, dark and all-seeing, brooking no resistance from me.

"He was again wearing black, this time a soft black shirt, with full sleeves and tight cuffs. His long black hair was tied back with a leather thong. He kissed my mouth, his lips soft against mine as I descended from the dizzying pinnacle of my orgasm. 'Come,' he said, 'let's go home.'

"Could I walk with this giant cock inside of me? I found that I could, and soon I was seated in his car, seat belt tightly fastened between my bared breasts. 'Close your eyes and think about your pussy,' he said as he started the engine. 'Feel how full it is and climb to the heights again.'

"I closed my eyes. My orgasm had been so hard and so complete that I wondered whether I could get excited again, but the dildo in my cunt gave me no peace. It aroused me as I pictured my swollen lips almost kissing the blunt end of it. By the time we pulled into the familiar garage, I was hungry again.

"He guided me from the car and into his special room. 'Remember last evening I showed you that frame,' he said, pointing to the X-shaped device that he was now moving to the center of the room. It was about six feet tall and each of the four arms was upholstered in black leather. There was a flat section at the center, against which my torso would be supported, I thought. As I looked more closely I saw that the frame had flat metal hinges and small metal rings at various points. He was going to fasten me to that, I knew, and control me totally. *Marshmallow,* I remembered was the magic word that would stop everything.

"'Strip,' he said. When I didn't immediately move, he glared at me. 'I told you to do something.'

"'Yes, Sir,' I said, quickly removing my clothing, my eyes still glued to the frame. As I pulled off my skirt, I saw the black leather harness wrapped around my body just above my hipbones, and fastened at the center-front with a tiny padlock. A leather panel held the dildo in place. Wasn't he going to remove it now?

"'Come here,' he said. It was a bit difficult to walk gracefully since the dildo held my legs slightly parted but I stepped forward and stood before him. 'I discovered last evening that a little pain gives you pleasure. You know it does, don't you?'

"I wanted to deny it. It was so sick. Wasn't it? But if both of us wanted it, and it gave us both pleasure . . . 'Yes, Sir.'

"'But the pain is just a symptom of what really excites you. It's the fact that I can do anything I want to you. I control you. I can hurt you or tease you and it's all pleasure for you. I can do anything, can't I?'

"'Yes, Sir.'

"'And you can always stop me. Snap your fingers or say *marshmallow* and I'll stop. So who's really in control?'

"I'd never thought of it that way before and now I couldn't keep a small smile from crossing my lips. 'We are, Sir,' I said.

"'And you trust me?'

"'Completely, Sir.'

"'Tonight there will be no pain, just a demonstration of what control means.' He enclosed me in his arms and softly kissed me. He slid his tongue into my mouth and I stroked it with mine. I wanted to feel him, hold him but I left my arms at my sides. If he wanted me to touch him, he would tell me. And he hadn't.

"He framed my face with his hands and kissed my cheeks, then walked to a chest, opened a drawer, and withdrew a handful of what looked to me like wide leather strips. He handed one to me. 'This goes around one ankle. Put it on.'

"I was going to have to do this myself. I was going to have to admit to myself that I wanted it. I took the strap and only hesitated a moment before I buckled it around my left ankle, leaving a large ring hanging from the back. I did the same with the one for my right ankle. Then my master gently buckled cuffs around my wrists. My master. Yes, that was what he was. He looked at the frame, then at me.

"Slowly I moved to the frame, pressed my back against it, raised my arms, and spread my legs. It fully supported my back but the leg sections parted at the small of my back, so there was nothing against my ass. Quickly, four small chains and padlocks fastened my arms and legs in place. 'Now,' he said, 'try to move. I want you to know how firmly you are held. I want you to know that now your body moves only when I adjust the frame.'

"I twisted and pulled, reveling in the feeling of being unable to free myself. 'Now you know how it feels. Tell me.'

"'It feels wonderful. It frees me.'

"He smiled as his hand reached between my legs. He tapped the end of the dildo and erotic pleasure knifed through my body. He twisted the plastic cock and moved it around as much as he could with the strap in place. I closed my eyes and clutched at the feeling of pleasure.

"He released the phallus inside me and moved the frame so it was now horizontal, at exactly the level of his groin. He unzipped his pants and allowed his cock to spring free. Then he moved so his hips were near my face, his engorged member near my mouth. 'Lick the tip,' he said. 'Just lick it with the tip of your tongue.' "

"God, you're good," Hector said. "I can almost feel what you were feeling."

Alice smiled and continued, her hand again snaking into the waist of her pants. "I reached out my tongue and touched the wet tip of my master's penis. Thick, sticky fluid oozed from the opening and I caught it on my tongue. While I licked, he reached over and pinched my nipples, hard. I gasped, but he said, 'Lick softly. Control your actions as I control the pleasure you feel.'

"It was difficult to lick his cock gently while he was pinching my nipples, but I managed. My mind was in two places at once, jumping from the feel of his fingers on my tight nipples to the movements of my mouth.

"Still twisting my nipples, he lifted a small handheld device and, while I watched, turned a small knob. 'Shit,' I hissed as the dildo inside my pussy began to hum. And the strap of the harness pressed against my clit so the vibrations were transferred to my engorged nub. Now my mind was in three places, my nipples, my tongue, and my pussy.

"'Control your actions,' he growled. 'Don't stop licking me.'

"'Oh,' I groaned, trying to concentrate on my tongue. I began to get used to the buzzing in my cunt, then he turned the knob and the frequency changed. Each time I became accustomed to the devilish object inside of me, he changed its method of torture, from buzzing to a slow throb, to a fast pounding and back to a low hum. And intermittently he pinched my nipples. Everything in my body was driving me closer and closer to orgasm, yet I was supposed to lick his penis in the same, soft rhythm.

"'Are you close to coming?' he asked.

"'Oh yes,' I moaned.

"'Don't! Just lick.'

"'But Sir.'

"'No buts. You will come only when I say you may. Do you understand?' He pushed his cock closer to my lips.

"'Yes, Sir.'

"'A lesson in control, yours and mine. Now,' he said, pushing his cock against my lips, 'take it.' "

"Are you close now, Sherry?" Hector asked. "I am."

Sherry's fingers rubbed her clit. "I am too," she said honestly.

"I like that. Continue with your story."

"I parted my lips and took the length of his engorged tool into my hot mouth. I ran my tongue over the sides, and created a vacuum to draw his penis more deeply into me. All the time my body sang with the sensations he was creating with his hands and with the machine in my pussy. If I can make him come, I reasoned, he will let me climax with him. I used every skill I possessed to drive him closer to orgasm.

"'You're very good at that,' he said, 'but I learned that last night. You're a good little cocksucker but I don't want to come this way.' He pulled away.

"I didn't know where the condom had come from but now he opened the small package and, as I watched, he slowly unrolled it over his cock. He walked around the frame until he was between my spread legs. 'Do you want this?' he asked.

"'Oh yes, Sir,' I said.

"He turned off the vibrating dildo, unfastened the strap that held it in place. And slowly withdrew it from my pussy. 'I control everything you feel,' he said, 'and I want you to feel everything. Have you ever taken something in your ass?'

"In my ass? He can't mean that. His cock was so big. He couldn't possibly do that. But I knew that he could. And if he wanted it that way, then he would do it. I couldn't stop him and I didn't want to. I wanted everything he could give me. 'No, Sir.'

"'Do you want your ass filled?'

"'No, Sir. I don't think so. It will hurt.'

"'It might, but it will be incredibly exciting as well. And you won't refuse me, will you. You really want anything that I think will please you. You realize that I know you better than you know yourself.'

"'Yes, Sir,' I said, and meant it.

"'So, now we understand each other. Your body is mine and I can do with it what I want.' Suddenly I felt something cold rubbing and pressing against my rear hole. 'I could drive my cock into you,' he said as the cold rubbing continued, driving me crazy with lust. 'But for now, we'll be content with this.' Something hard was pressing against my anus, slowly slipping into the tight ring of muscle. He alternately pressed and remained still so my body could become accustomed to the unfamiliar sensation.

"For moments at a time, it hurt, and I considered saying *marshmallow* but just as the pain got too much, he stopped pushing and the discomfort subsided. Finally my ass was filled and the pain had disappeared to be replaced with heat deep in my belly. He withdrew the object and pushed it in again, fucking me with it. While my mind was centered on my ass, he inserted his cock into my pussy. He quickly established a mind-blowing rhythm, inserting his cock and withdrawing the dildo, then reversing, so one of my openings was filled while the other was empty and hungry.

"'I'm stroking my cock with the dildo, through your body,' he said. 'And we are going to come together.' Harder and harder, faster and faster, he pumped both his cock and the rod until I knew he was ready to climax. Although we both knew I was close, how was he going to create the moment? I wondered with the small bit of my brain still capable of coherent thought. I was so close that I didn't think I could delay or speed my climax. Could he control the timing?

"I needn't have worried. Suddenly his finger was on my clit and I came. 'Yes,' I screamed and wave after wave of orgasmic pleasure overwhelmed my body. I couldn't move my arms or my legs but I bucked my hips as much as possible, taking his cock as deeply into my body as I could."

Alice smiled as she realized that when the character in the story came, she did too. She was even controlling her own orgasm.

"And he screamed as well, loudly proclaiming his pleasure. Over and over he pounded his cock into me, fucking my ass with the dildo as well.

"My climax was the strongest and longest as I could

ever remember. Wave upon wave of erotic joy washed over me and just as I thought I was descending, I came again. After several minutes of almost unendurable pleasure, I began to calm.

"A long time passed before our breathing returned to almost normal. Slowly he pulled the rod from my ass and then withdrew his cock from me. Then, leaving me to compose my body, he sat in a chair, his eyes closed, his body limp and trembling. 'God, lady,' he said, 'you're amazing.'

"'You too,' I said, unable to move even if I hadn't been still fastened to the frame.

"'And this is only the beginning.'

"'Yes,' I said, then added, 'Sir.'"

"Wow," Hector said.

Alice was unsure whether Hector had come. "Are you all right?"

"I'm terrific. I came about two minutes ago," he said, "but I stayed silent so I could hear you talk. You're sensational."

Alice grinned, and at that moment she knew that she couldn't do it. She couldn't leave Velvet Whispers. She enjoyed it too much. To hell with the medical coverage. To hell with security. She'd leave Dr. Tannenbaum as soon as he could find someone else and continue to do the things that she most enjoyed, and phone sex was at the top of her list. She'd stay at Velvet Whispers as long as she loved it and the men kept calling.

"I'm glad you think so. Call me next week?"

"Sure. Can you tell me what you and that guy did on a different night?"

"Of course I can. I'll talk to you next week."

She was about to call Velvet to tell her about her change of heart when the phone rang. "Alice, I'm in a jam," Velvet said quickly. Without allowing Alice to interrupt, Velvet continued, "I know Hector was your last caller but Marie just threw up. I can reroute all of her calls but I've already got a new client on the line and I promised him someone special. Everyone else is on the phone right now and I'm routing so I can't take him. Can you do me a favor, just one last time?"

"I'm not leaving. I've changed my mind."

"Thanks for taking this one last . . . You're not leaving?"

"Of course not. I was being ridiculous. I can't leave all my friends without anyone to talk to. And they are my friends even though I've never seen them. I'll give Dr. Tannenbaum my notice in the morning."

She could hear Velvet's laugh. "I knew you'd come to your senses. You love this as much as I do. Does Betsy know yet?"

"I just hung up with Hector and he made the decision for me. He said, 'Next week?' and I just said, 'Sure.' "

"Let's have lunch, the three of us, tomorrow to celebrate. I'll even buy."

"That will be great. Now, you said you had a new client?"

"His name is Zack and he's interested in telling you about his wild date last evening. He was babbling about a video camera and several mirrors. I don't know whether your story-telling talents will be needed, so just go with the flow."

"Will do." A few moments later her phone rang. "Sherry? This is Zack."

Alice lowered her voice, stretched out on the bed, and flipped off the light. "Hi, Zack. I'm glad you called."

Dear Reader,

I hope you've enjoyed the adventures of Alice, Betsy, and Velvet as much as I enjoyed writing them. Maybe I'll revisit the Velvet Whispers phone service again in a future book.

If you enjoyed the short stories that Alice read and her adventures on the phone, please read my other books, and visit my Web site at http://www.JoanELloyd.com. I know you'll love all my characters and their antics.

I'd love to hear from you anytime, so drop me a note and let me know what you particularly enjoyed and what you would like to read about in a future book. Please write me at:

Joan E. Lloyd
P.O. Box 221
Yorktown Heights, NY 10598

or at: JoanELloyd@aol.com.